SAVING US

A.D. ELLIS

To Felice for her beautiful stories and for allowing me to write in her world.
And, thank you to Donna. Your story touched my heart. For all the Roy's out there.

1

"Look, *Officer*, it's creeping me out that you're practically stalking me." Jamie Abbott tossed his light brown hair from his forehead and sneered at John Kirkland while wiping down a table at the popular, cozy little restaurant where he was a new employee. "I mean, thanks for getting me the job. I appreciate your cop connections with Sam and all, and it was super helpful for him and his buddies to put in a good word for me, but you've been here pretty much every day this week. Maybe you should do the old guy creeper routine somewhere else or focus on someone who's maybe the slightest bit interested."

Jamie kept up the act of washing the table throughout his diatribe. Officer John "Kirk" Kirkland bit the inside of his cheek to keep from laughing at the kid's tantrum. "So, you admit you've noticed me?" Kirk smirked.

"Kinda hard *not* to notice you. You're in a uniform, with your big bad gun and shiny badge, drinking like five gallons of coffee and staring at me." Jamie finally stopped wiping the table. Lucky for the table because he'd almost rubbed a hole in it. "Like I said, CREEP-EEE." Jamie threw a glance over his shoulder at a table of six men. "At least go sit with your friends so you don't look like some loser."

"Sam is a former police department colleague, but we've not been close since he moved into the private investigator job." Kirk gave a quick nod and friendly wave toward the table of men when he noticed them failing miserably to look like they weren't watching his interaction with Jamie. "I don't know the other guys well, just by name and appearance. I think one is a fashion designer. The one with his back to us used to be with the fire department, not sure if he still is. Nick something or other is his name, I think. The suave looking one owns Sparks nightclub. No clue who the guy next to him is. The geeky one is maybe with Sam, but I'm not one hundred percent on that either." Kirk shrugged and sipped his coffee.

"Gee, thanks for the who's who rundown, Officer. Now, can you leave?" Jamie glanced toward the clock. "I gotta get back to work."

"Where you staying?" Kirk asked and secretly admired Jamie's dusty blue eyes.

"Yeah, like I'm dumb enough to fall for that one." Jamie rolled his eyes. "Don't worry, Old Man, I'm with friends."

"Yeah," Kirk scoffed, "like *I'm* going to fall for that."

"I got it covered," Jamie spoke through gritted teeth.

"That why you've had on the same shirt three days in a row?" Kirk interrogated criminals for a living. The kid didn't have a chance.

"Just haven't had time to do laundry." Jamie lifted a shoulder but his gaze flitted down to the worn toes of his shoes.

"You've been on your own for over a week," Kirk started.

"Don't. Don't remind me of that night." Jamie's face flushed and his nostrils flared. "I get it. You saw me at my worst, and you know my situation is fucked up. But I'm not your damn charity case. You did your job and rescued me. You're the fucking hero. But I don't owe you shit, man."

Jamie started away from the table but came to a dead stop when Kirk gently grabbed his wrist. "Jamie, stop."

"Let. Go. Of. Me." Jamie spit out each word.

Kirk released Jamie's wrist immediately. "Just hear me out. I know what's it like to be alone, scared," he lowered his voice slightly, "and *gay*. Come home with me after your shift."

Jamie shot Kirk a look of disgusted disbelief. "Yeah, that's not going to happen. I'm not some fuckin' rent boy."

"That's not what I meant, you little smartass. Come home with me, do some laundry, and take a shower. *Alone*. Eat some decent food and sleep in a decent bed. Again, *alone*." Kirk watched as emotions ranging from longing to shame to anger flitted across Jamie's face.

"I get food here." Jamie jutted out his chin.

"Do you get to do laundry here?" Kirk eyed the three-day-old stains on the hem of Jamie's shirt.

"No," Jamie muttered. "Fine. I'll use your washing machine and take a shower. But I'm not agreeing to staying over. You may have sworn to protect and serve, but that doesn't mean I want any part in your serving now that you've done your duty to protect me."

"What time do you get off?" Kirk ignored the kid's insults.

"An hour."

"You got your stuff with you, or do you need to pick it up?"

Jamie mumbled something unintelligible.

"What was that?" Kirk cocked his head.

"I *said* my stuff's at the teen center. Got someone watching it for me." Jamie huffed.

"Thought you were staying with *friends*?" Kirk drawled.

"Yeah, well, maybe the people at the teen center are the only *friends* I got right about now," Jamie whispered.

"Not true." Kirk stared at him. "You got me. You could probably ask any of the little Breakfast Club crew over there for help in a pinch too. Maybe even your boss here at the restaurant. I'm glad you've got the teen center to turn to because they're good people, but that doesn't give you a place to sleep."

"I get by." Jamie once again turned to walk away.

"I'll be out front in an hour," Kirk called after him.

Jamie shrugged as he disappeared around a corner.

Kirk just shook his head.

"Kid looks like he's got a huge chip on his shoulder," Sam Stein said from Kirk's left side.

Kirk had been so wrapped up in watching and thinking about Jamie, he hadn't even noticed Sam and another man approach.

"More like a boulder," Kirk grunted. He stood and shook hands with Sam. "Good to see you again, man. Thanks for helping the kid out. I won't go into his personal affairs, but he was in a rough situation and really needed this job."

Sam returned the handshake. "No problem. I'm glad we could help. The people here are good folk, and they'll treat him fairly." Sam put his arm around the man who stood at his side. "Wanted to introduce you to my partner, Zach Cohen. Zach, this is Kirk."

Zach offered a warm smile and shook Kirk's hand.

"Nice to meet you." Zach nodded.

"You, too," Kirk responded.

"Well, we need to head out. Just wanted to say hello. We've seen you in here a lot lately. Thought it would be rude to continue to just wave from across the room." Sam smiled.

"Yeah, I've been worried about the kid." Kirk's gaze traveled to the kitchen door Jamie had disappeared behind.

"He seems a bit prickly," Zach ventured.

"You have no idea." Kirk chuckled darkly. "But he's pretty much on his own and going through a hell of a lot right now. Doesn't feel right to turn my back on him."

"Remember what we learned on the force," Sam reminded. "We can't save them all."

Kirk gave a small smile. "Nah, I know. But doesn't mean I won't try."

2

Jamie slunk from the front door, head down, hood up, shoulders hunched and made his way toward the corner without so much as a glance toward Kirk's unmarked patrol car. Which led Kirk to believe that the kid had scoped him out from inside and decided to ignore him by attempting to sneak away.

Kirk shook his head, put the car in gear, and pulled from the parking lot at a crawl to keep pace with Jamie. The kid was so damn cute. Angry, scared, and hurting. But fuck, he was cute. Kirk continued to follow Jamie while his mind wandered to his own angry, scared, and hurt-filled youth.

Kirk had never had the courage to come out at that age. No, he hid. Pretended to be someone he wasn't. Took the easy way out, which was best for him at that point in his life. However, looking back, he wondered just how much time he'd wasted.

Jamie was from a prominent right-wing conservative background. From what Kirk had gathered when he'd been called to the domestic dispute about a week earlier, Jamie had lived a stifled life until he went off to college on his parents' dime. The kid quickly found friends in the campus LGBTQ community and began living as a gay man. A video of Jamie kissing another man made its way to social media and, thanks to face recognition technology, Jamie was tagged. A cousin with whom Jamie had always butted heads saw the video and outed Jamie while he was home on a break from school.

Kirk's eyes never left Jamie's long, lean body as he loped down the sidewalk, head down, hands in his pockets. Would Kirk have been brave enough to admit his sexuality in the same circumstances? As it was, Jamie refused to claim he was heterosexual as his parents had demanded. So they took away his college education money. By the time the neighbors had called the police, Jamie's dad had physically tossed his son down the stairs. When Kirk and his partner pulled up to the scene, Kirk's stomach sank. Jamie, curled into a ball to protect his midsection, had looked like a young boy huddled on the sidewalk as his dad frothed at the mouth and screeched about his good family name, their position in society, and how God would punish Jamie if he didn't repent.

Now, Jamie stopped on the sidewalk and stalked toward Kirk's car, effectively breaking the officer from his memories of that horrific night. Jamie leaned down to look into the car through the passenger side window. "Look, Officer Creepy Pants, I've decided I really don't like you that much. You can go on home, I'll be fine."

Kirk noticed the kid's shiver and the lost look in his eyes. "Listen, you little shit, just get in the car. Do some laundry, take a shower, and eat. If you don't want to get a good night's sleep, that's your choice. It's cold tonight, so don't be stubborn."

Jamie's eyes narrowed. "How do I know you're not just a uniformed pedophile looking to prey on young boys?"

"Well, for one, the department frowns upon their officers having criminal tendencies or arrest records." Kirk reached over and yanked the handle to push open the door. "Second, you're nineteen, so even if I was looking to prey on you it wouldn't make me a pedophile."

Jamie climbed into the car, shivered again in the cold, and removed his hood. "Those are terrible arguments." He crossed both arms over his chest after putting on his seatbelt.

"Don't worry, kid. I don't *prey on* men who don't reciprocate the attraction. You're safe." Kirk turned a corner and headed toward the teen center. He and many in his department volunteered there a couple times a week when their shifts and personal lives allowed. Since Kirk's personal life had gone to shit not too long ago, he found himself volunteering at the center more and more. He found his time at the center a great way to relax, build relationships with the community, and forget his troubles for a while. Many of the kids at the teen center were dealing with a lot more than he was at twenty-nine.

"I mean, you're not ugly," Jamie sassed. "You just need a new hobby. Preferably one that doesn't include babysitting me."

"Gee, thanks for the compliment." Kirk chuckled. "Maybe I'll put that on my Grindr profile. *Twenty-nine, officer of the law, not ugly.* I bet that would draw in some real winners."

"Dude, you gotta be careful on Grindr." Jamie shot him a serious look. "I mean it. There are some damn fucked up people out there." Jamie paused for a moment. "I mean, maybe you're into that sort of thing?"

Kirk couldn't tell if the kid was fishing or truly just offering advice. "Nah, I'm not into fucked up stuff. Some whips and chains in my basement. Maybe some diaper play." He nearly broke his teeth keeping a straight face.

"The fuck you say," Jamie yelped as he scrambled to get off his seatbelt. "I knew this was a bad idea."

"Calm down, kiddo. I'm joking." Kirk lifted a hand from the steering wheel to halt Jamie's actions. "I'm likely one of the most vanilla gay guys you'll ever meet. I'm out, but not shouting it from the rooftops. I've been on a few good dates and some really disastrous ones. I'm a romantic at heart, love to hold hands and cuddle, and have pretty much accepted I'll never find *the one*."

Kirk's words spilled from his mouth like vomit from a hungover perp. Why in the world was he telling this kid so much personal information?

Jamie squinted. "Is this where you get me to trust you so you can rape, kill, and dismember me?"

"Damn, you've got issues." Kirk shook his head. "I just told you I'm basically a sap, I'm not into the kinky shit—at least that I know about—and my love life is pathetic. I have no plans to rape you, kill you, *or* dismember you." Kirk pulled into the teen center. "Can I trust you to get your stuff and come back out or do I need to go in with you?"

"Now who has the trust issues, Officer?" Jamie quipped. "I'll come back. I'm beginning to think you're even more fucked up than I am. Maybe I can make myself feel better by hanging out with you for a while." He launched himself from the car.

Kirk couldn't keep his gaze from the swagger and sway of Jamie's hips, and the way the wind tossed his floppy brown hair. Being attracted to a man was nothing new. Being attracted to a man ten years his junior was definitely new and probably not a good idea. Being attracted to a kid he knew through a police call and the teen center was *definitely* not a good idea.

Shit.

Then why did Kirk feel such a damn draw to the kid? Why such a longing to protect him? Why such an attraction to Jamie? Kirk had dealt with plenty of suspects and victims through work and at the center. He'd never once felt an ounce of desire toward *any* of them. What the hell was so different about Jamie?

Jamie loped from the center with his knapsack thrown over his shoulder and his eyes sparkling. He threw his bag in the back and hopped in the front. "Let's go, Officer, I'm hungry and these clothes ain't gonna wash themselves."

Kirk had a sinking feeling he'd gotten in way over his head. But the flush in Jamie's cheeks, the brightness in his eyes—something Kirk hadn't seen before—he way Kirk's heart longed to reach out and hold the kid told him he couldn't remove himself from the situation.

He was too far-gone.

3

Jamie glanced around Kirk's place in Carroll Gardens. The townhouse seemed like way too much for a single guy on a cop's salary. "Wow, guess cops are getting paid a lot more these days than I thought."

"Nah, I got the place way before this area became the hip and cool place to live. Did quite a bit of fixing up. It's not the biggest or the best, but it's home." Kirk tossed his keys on the hallway table. "You want a tour?"

Jamie shrugged. The kid's shoulder muscles were likely incredibly toned from the number of shoulder shrugs he did.

"So, the whole basement is sort of a wasteland right now. We'll skip it." Kirk pointed toward the basement door.

"Sure, sure. No need to show me where you hide the bodies." Jamie smirked.

Kirk ignored him. "Bathroom is here. Towels, soap, and all that is in the closet. You saw the kitchen when we came in. Master bedroom and bath is to the right. Guest bedroom up the hall and to the left. Laundry is out back in the utility room."

"It's a nice place." Jamie nodded. "Guess I never really thought much about having a place to stay until I didn't. My parents' house was ridiculously extravagant. My college dorm was amazingly simple and compact and perfect because it was my own space. No clue how I'll ever afford a place to live now." Jamie frowned as he looked around the house.

"Well, my offer stands. You're welcome to stay here as long as needed." Kirk grabbed Jamie's bag and walked it to the utility room. He paused and turned to wait for Jamie.

"Why? What's in it for you?" Jamie narrowed his eyes.

"Just knowing I'm helping you out of a bind." It was Kirk's turn to shrug.

"Aren't you just a saint?" Jamie rolled his eyes. "You got anything I can wear after a shower while my clothes wash?"

"Yeah, may be a bit big in the waist but we're about the same height so I think my stuff will work." Kirk disappeared into the master bedroom and returned with a roll of clothing. "Use anything in the bathroom. Holler if there's something you need that you don't find. I'll fix some food."

JAMIE LEANED AGAINST THE SHOWER'S TILE WALL AND LET THE HOT water rain down as his tears scalded down his face.

He'd never needed anything from anyone. Open and honest communication and love hadn't been present in his home, but he'd never wanted for material items such as clothing, shelter, or food.

Now he was in way over his head. Beaten and then kicked out by his father, he knew his dreams of college were torn away unless he denounced his sexuality. The beginnings of friendships and relationships in college were a distant memory. With no money to travel to campus and get his belongings, Jamie could only hope his roommate would ship some of his personal items.

Homeless, hungry, beaten, scared, and alone.

Jamie had been confused and frightened as he figured out his sexuality in his early teen years. But he'd never been as scared and alone as he was now. New York City was a cold ass mother fucker at this time of the year. The God his parents had shoved down his throat must have been smiling down on Jamie to provide him with a good job so quickly after his disownment. Food was an issue sometimes, but the restaurant job meant he wouldn't starve to death. But sleeping in dark doorways, in the alley outside of the teen center, or on random couches for a night at a time was getting really old, really fast.

The hot water eased his sore muscles. The scent of soap filled the air as he lathered and rinsed not once but twice. He repeated the lathering and rinsing procedure with shampoo in his hair. He didn't want to get out of the shower, but using up all of Officer Kirkland's hot water would be rude.

What was it about the man that rubbed Jamie the wrong way? Kirkland was drop dead gorgeous, but he didn't seem to realize how attractive he was. He didn't have that swagger or conceited air about him that some men did. Jamie was beyond grateful the man had rescued him from the lowest point in his short nineteen years of life. And having Kirk understand at least a little bit of what Jamie was going through was helpful. But Jamie's pride was getting in the way.

Fact: Kirk was extending generosity and kindness in his offer to help Jamie.

Fact: Kirk understood what it was like to be the scared and alone gay guy among a sea of homophobic bastards.

Fact: Kirk was a fucking wet dream on legs.

Fact: Jamie's head and heart were at war with his libido and dick.

On one hand, Jamie wanted to climb Officer Kirkland like a fucking tree and let him do all sorts of dirty things. On the other hand, Jamie felt the sting of humiliation every time he recalled Kirk hefting Jamie's bruised and bloody body from the sidewalk and helping him into the patrol car. Jamie had never taken charity, never needed a handout, or a hand up. It felt like complete and utter failure to admit he was at rock bottom.

But Jamie wouldn't let his pride keep him from taking advantage of Kirk's food and laundry facilities. The shower had been spectacular and a warm bed was beyond tempting. Maybe he'd think more clearly after eating.

Enjoying the soft warmth of the fluffy towel as he dried himself, Jamie rummaged through the linen closet until he found an unopened toothbrush and a stick of deodorant. He put them both to use before pulling up the borrowed loose boxers and slipping into the soft sweatpants and even softer long sleeve t-shirt. Sliding on the socks, Jamie caught a whiff of deodorant, maybe detergent, and groaned at how much he enjoyed the scent he'd already begun to associate with Kirk.

Maybe spending the night and getting good sleep wouldn't be so bad after all. Relief and sleepiness warmed his body as much as the shower had.

A knock sounded at the door. "Food's ready whenever you are," Kirk's deep voice traveled through the wood.

"Be right out." Jamie gathered up his dirty clothing and towel before opening the door. A cool blast of air hit his still damp skin and hair causing him to shiver. He walked the pile of laundry to the utility room before returning to the kitchen where Kirk was pulling a pizza from the oven. Jamie's mouth watered.

"Grab some waters from the fridge." Kirk placed the pizza pan on the stovetop before reaching back into the oven for breadsticks. "We'll use paper plates if that's okay with you."

Within moments, the table was set with paper and plastic, and Jamie had to fight against his stomach's demand that he devour the entire spread of food in mere seconds.

"Dig in." Kirk smiled as he lifted a cheesy slice of pizza to his mouth.

Jamie forced himself to chug half his water before eating the first bite.

"Thirsty?" Kirk went to the refrigerator and got Jamie another water.

"Thanks," Jamie mumbled. "I try to drink as much water as possible so I don't get sick or dehydrated."

"You been feeling bad?" Kirk frowned.

Jamie rolled his eyes. "No, just realized earlier in the week that I likely no longer have medical insurance. I'm sure Dad took that away, too. Can't afford a doctor, so I'm trying to stay healthy."

"Smart." Kirk nodded and returned to his pizza. "They let you keep water at work?"

"Yeah, I can keep a bottle filled and in the breakroom so I can take drinks all shift." Jamie finished his first piece and fiddled with his napkin.

"Grab some more." Kirk nodded toward the pizza. "No way I'm eating this whole monster by myself."

Jamie reached for another slice. "Thanks. Didn't realize how hungry I was."

"You gotta make sure you're eating enough along with the water. What about vitamins? You should get some. And a heavier coat and hat." Kirk rambled his list of concerns.

"Slow down, *Dad*," Jamie snarked. "You got kids?"

Kirk shook his head.

"Okay then, I don't think you need to be going all parental on me. I'm nineteen, an adult. I can take care of myself." Jamie demolished the last of his pizza and stood to throw away his trash.

"Didn't seem that way from my end of things." Kirk bit out and winced almost before the words had even left his lips.

"You know what? Fuck you." Jamie jabbed at Kirk's chest with his finger before heading to the utility room.

"Jamie, wait. That wasn't fair. I'm sorry," Kirk hollered down the hallway.

"Fuck off." Jamie picked up his bag of dirty clothes and threw them into the washer along with the clothes he'd been wearing for at least three days. He doused the clothing with detergent and slammed shut the lid. Staring in confusion at the machine that was so different from the washers in his dormitory, Jamie searched the control panel for something resembling *WASH*.

"Here, let me." Kirk reached around Jamie and turned a few knobs. "Want them washed in hot?"

Kirk's words fell mere inches from Jamie's ear and his warm breath caused a chill to travel along Jamie's skin. "Hot is fine," Jamie mumbled, trying to ignore the heat Kirk's proximity sent through his body.

Without removing himself from the warmth of Jamie's body, Kirk continued. "I'm sorry about what I said. I'm trying to help, and when you struck out at me, I reflexively struck out at you. You have nothing to be ashamed of. Your parents were wrong. You're better off without hateful people in your life." Jamie savored the heat radiating from Kirk's body for one more second before the man took a slight step away.

Jamie turned and stared at Kirk. His cheeks were flushed and his breathing was heavy.

Was it because he was angry?

Or was he as turned on as Kirk?

"I'll never be able to forget the pain of hatred and the sting of humiliation from that night. But it would be really great if you'd never rub it in again." Jamie's nostril's flared as he spoke.

"You got it." Kirk nodded. "Again, I'm sorry."

Jamie glanced at the washing machine. "How long does this thing take to run a cycle?"

Kirk raised a shoulder. "Never really thought about it. You can probably have the entire load washed and dried in an hour and a half, two hours tops."

Jamie shuffled his feet. "Okay, sounds good." He crossed both arms across his chest and leaned against the washer. "Don't think you gotta babysit me. I'll be fine."

Jamie's words were clearly meant to dismiss Kirk or let him off the hook.

Kirk smiled. "Didn't figure you needed babysitting, but you can't hang out in my utility room for two hours. Come on in while the load washes."

Jamie gave Kirk a look that proved the kid wasn't that far out of his attitudinal teen years and then he shouldered past before shuffling to the living room.

Kirk followed. "You can have the couch. The recliner is mine." Kirk flopped down into his favorite worn leather chair.

"That thing looks like you've had it since *you* were in college," Jamie scoffed as he sat on the far end of the couch and tucked his long legs under himself.

"You're not far off." Kirk rubbed his hands lovingly along the soft leather. "She may not be much to look at, but she's gotten me through many a night, many an illness, and many a good movie."

"No way my mom would have *ever* let my dad keep a chair like that in the house." Jamie chuckled. "Not that my dad would ever lower himself by having a chair like that."

"To each his own." Kirk turned on the television. "You like anything in particular?"

"Nah, I gave up any hope of keeping up with shows I used to watch. Maybe the news or weather so I know what's going on and what to expect?" Jamie yawned while making his suggestions.

"Here, make yourself comfortable." Kirk leaned forward and to his left to reach into a large wooden chest between his chair and the couch. He pulled out a soft, plush blanket.

"I'm good." Jamie shook his head.

"Dude, you've got time while you wait for the wash. Rest for a bit." Kirk threw the blanket at Jamie's head.

Jamie huffed and batted at the blanket. But he spread it out over his legs and cuddled down a bit deeper into the corner of the couch.

Kirk flipped to a local news station and pulled the lever to recline his chair.

Within five minutes, Kirk heard a soft snore from Jamie's end of the sofa. Torn between protective feelings and attraction, Kirk watched the kid sleep. Then while enjoying the comfortable silence and knowing Jamie was safe for the time being, Kirk closed his eyes.

Just for a second.

Jamie woke with a start and glanced around to get his bearings. He'd been sleeping in cramped, cold, unfamiliar places for over a week and waking up confused was his new norm.

The sound of soft breathing came from Jamie's right, and he immediately recognized Kirk who was stretched out in the recliner. Shower, food, laundry—and nothing more. No matter the attraction, Jamie had too much on his plate to even entertain getting involved with the officer who likely only viewed Jamie as a damsel in distress.

But Kirk *had* offered a place to stay.

Kirk seemed to be sending the same *I want you, but I shouldn't* vibes that were right in line with Jamie's.

Jamie's resolve waivered.

No.

Kirk had seen Jamie at his all-time lowest of lows. Jamie had no intention of staying with a guy with a hero complex who probably looked at Jamie as a pathetic rescue case.

Kirk had basically said exactly that earlier when he'd slipped up during dinner.

Jamie stood quietly and folded the blanket before heading to the kitchen to down some more water. Damn, he needed to piss.

After taking care of business, Jamie went to the utility room. Pleased to find his clothes done in the washer, he switched them to the dryer, throwing in a dryer sheet and picking the hottest setting possible in hopes of getting out of Kirk's house quickly.

By the time he'd returned to the living room, Kirk had awakened and had waters and cookies on the coffee table.

"Thought you might want a snack. The cookies are from a bakery nearby. Like, legit homemade goodness." Kirk pushed the plate of assorted cookies toward Jamie.

Jamie picked up a frosted treat and moaned as his teeth sank into the soft, sugary sinfulness. "Oh my god, that's good."

"Right? Told ya." Kirk grabbed his own cookie and chomped into it. "Your mom a baker? Cook?"

"Yeah, she was really good at baking and cooking. Kind of always felt like Dad only married her because she could play Susie Homemaker for him. They only had me. Lost a couple babies after. I think Dad always blamed Mom for not being able to give him a passel of kids. You know, the whole 'keep her barefoot and pregnant at home' type mentality. That's my Dad to a T." Jamie finished one cookie and selected a soft and chewy Snickerdoodle for his next. "I think Mom always felt guilty so she doubled up on housecleaning and baked goods and having dinner ready when Dad got home. She was like a nineteen fifties housewife. And I was pretty much to be seen and not heard. Don't speak unless spoken to." Jamie was silent for a moment. "It worries me to think of Dad taking his anger out on Mom. Like blaming her for 'making me gay.'"

Kirk sat quietly for a moment in case Jamie wanted to continue his train of thought.

"You have a hard time being gay on a police force?" Jamie blushed as he took a third cookie, the kid's stomach obviously winning over any embarrassment.

The abrupt subject change was a cue that any discussion regarding Jamie's family issues was over for the time being apparently. Kirk stirred and mumbled, "Not really."

"Huh. I would have thought there'd be at least a little push-back." Jamie frowned and wiped a crumb from his lip.

"Little bit from the people who know." Kirk looked away and opened a bottle of water.

Jamie's eyes grew wide. "The people who know? And how many people *know* you're gay, Officer Kirkland?"

Kirk rolled his eyes and squirmed a bit before taking a drink.

"Well?" Jamie prompted.

"I mean, the vast majority of my family knows," Kirk muttered.

"But how many people at work?"

"My partner, the officer who rode with me the other day, he's a rookie and is completely cool with it."

"Awww, ain't that sweet?" Jamie mocked. "Who else?"

"My captain, but he chooses to pretend like it doesn't exist."

"And?"

"Two or three others," Kirk mumbled under his breath.

"I'm sorry, I couldn't hear that, could you repeat it please?" Jamie stared at Kirk with a look of disbelief.

"Two or three others. That's it." Kirk grimaced. "I'm not totally closeted at work, I just don't go around singing show tunes and waving pride flags."

"So, Officer Creepster, who wants me to be proud of standing up to my parents even though it meant getting my ass handed to me on a platter with a double side of degradation and humiliation, is basically a closet case at work? Oh, that's rich!" Jamie threw himself back against the couch. "So, the guy who is all worried about my protection and is concerned I can't take care of myself doesn't have the balls to be true to himself at work?"

Kirk frowned. "It's not that easy."

"Right, right. I get it. I can get the shit beat out of me after I'm outed by a jealous cousin and refusing to denounce my sexuality, but it's *too hard* for you to let people you work with know you like cock." Jamie huffed and rubbed his hands against his pants.

"Totally fine for you to see me in the fetal position on the sidewalk getting a boot to the ribs, but it's just too difficult for you to own up to who you really are with your colleagues."

Kirk shook his head. "There's still *a lot* of prejudice and homophobia and hatred. I patrol some of the worst parts of New York City daily. I need to know the people I work with have my back. Not just the ones who are okay with me being gay, but *all* of them."

Jamie was silent for a moment. "I still think it sucks you're hiding who you are. But it sucks even more that you have to. You should be able to trust your fellow officers." Jamie's anger relented a bit.

"Yeah, it does suck." Kirk picked up another cookie. "And you're right. I *should* be able to trust my colleagues. In a perfect world, I guess."

Kirk finished his cookie and watched as Jamie ate the last cookie from the plate during the next several silent moments.

"You planning on working full time now?" Kirk changed the subject this time.

"For now, yeah. Try to save some money." Jamie nodded. "But I can't give up my plans. And my plans include college."

"Yeah, what's your major?"

"Undecided right now, just getting a lot of prerequisites out of the way." Jamie fiddled with a string on his sweatpants. "But I don't plan on working retail or food service or making minimum wage forever. I'm going to do better, be better. With or without my parents' help."

"Good for you. You seem to be the type who will purposely make something out of yourself just to spite your parents." Kirk winked.

"Well, as much as I'd like to get pissy about you pretending to know *anything* about me, I'd have to agree with you on that one." Jamie smirked. "I will most definitely turn this into something successful, even if it almost kills me, especially if it means I get to throw it in my parents' faces."

Kirk smiled. "There ya go. At least you have a goal."

Jamie nodded. "I better check my clothes." He stood and walked toward the utility room.

Kirk's gaze followed Jamie's tight ass as it disappeared down the hall. Leaning back against the recliner, Kirk sighed. "Why does it have to be *him* I'm so damn attracted to? Why can't it be some nice, calm, thirty-ish guy who is settled into a career and isn't so damn prickly?"

4

J amie pulled pieces of laundry from the dryer one at a time
and folded them neatly before placing them in his bag.
The scent of freshly laundered clothing was something
Jamie never realized he'd miss.

As he reached for the last few odds and ends, Jamie's eyes
widened to find his hand filled with a pair of silky lace panties.

He held the scrap of silk and studied it from side to side. The
article looked much too small to be Kirk's, but then whose was it?
Kirk enjoyed wearing women's clothing? Or Kirk had a girlfriend?
Both options were more than Jamie's scrambled brain was willing
to grasp at that point.

Maybe Kirk had a male friend who wore lingerie.

A throat cleared behind him. "Um, I can explain those." Kirk's
voice held a heavy trace of guilty panic.

"Yeah? I didn't know you were a cross dresser. Or maybe drag?
No worries, I'm open minded." Jamie dangled the panties
between him and Kirk. "We all like to look pretty from time to
time."

Kirk yanked the panties from Jamie's hand. "I'm not a cross
dresser, and I don't do drag."

"Please don't tell me you're a gay guy who judges that type of thing."

"No, I don't judge that type of thing."

"Okay, so whose panties are in your dryer, Officer?" Jamie batted his lashes and waited not-so-patiently for Kirk to answer.

"They're my wife's," Kirk started and held up a hand to stave off Jamie's explosion.

"Your *wife*? You have a *wife*?" Jamie's eyes bulged from his head. "You're asking me to stay here, letting me shower, acting like you're my gay savior super hero, and you have a *wife*? Holy fuck, this is beyond fucked up. *You* are fucked up. Does wifey like to watch? Or maybe she fantasizes about being in between? So you're not really gay, you're bi?" Jamie stuffed the rest of his clothing into his knapsack throughout his diatribe.

By the time he'd run out of steam, Kirk was leaning against the wall with both arms crossed over his chest. "You finished?"

"Yeah, I'm finished. Done. Finito. Outta here." Jamie moved as if to leave the utility room, but Kirk stepped in front of him.

"You are *not* outta here. I meant, are you finished with your temper tantrum?" Kirk cocked his head and waited for Jamie to answer.

Jamie glared daggers at Kirk and jutted out his jaw.

"The underwear belong to my *ex-wife*."

"So? You're still sleeping with her, right? She lives here, and what? You're bi? Or just one of those straight guys hoping to get his dick sucked by a cute little homo?"

"I mean, while I agree you're a super cute little homo, and I definitely wouldn't mind...that. *No,* I'm not sleeping with my ex-wife, and I'm not bi."

Kirk's words came across as a mixture of frustrated and flirty. "But she *does* still live here, yes?"

"We're divorced."

"Just a little sex on the side?"

"Would you just listen for a second?"

Jamie narrowed his eyes, but stopped talking.

"Bethany and I were good friends growing up. Dating her was easy and comfortable and we moved into marriage just as easily."

"Such a sweet love story," Jamie snarked.

Kirk pinned the kid with a stare and continued. "Five years into our marriage, Bethany came to me and said she loved me but couldn't keep our marriage together when she knew I wasn't happy."

Jamie pursed his lips, but kept his mouth shut.

"She said she believed I was gay since high school, but she always thought I'd come around to accepting it on my own." Kirk leaned heavily against the doorframe. "She felt so guilty that she'd gone ahead with the marriage when her heart knew the truth." Kirk sighed. "Long story short, we are great friends and truly love each other, but being in a marriage wasn't fair to either of us. We've been divorced for about a year. At first, it made sense for her to stay until she found the right place, but then her mom got sick so she went to stay with her for several months. Now that her mom is doing better, Bethany is waiting for the tenants to vacate her new apartment. She's got most of her stuff in storage, but some of her clothes and other things are still here."

"Well, that's quite the story. Glad your wife had to tell you you're gay. Glad you're practically still in the closet at work. Glad you're a savior and saint and hero and all that." Jamie hitched his bag up on his shoulder. "But I've got way too much on my plate to deal with right now. I'm not in the market for a closeted crazy and his honey bunch." Jamie turned on his heel and bolted for the backdoor. "Thanks for the help. Really do appreciate it. See ya around, but don't worry about me."

Kirk stared at the door as Jamie trotted down the back steps.

The kid was probably right. The two of them were not at the same places in their lives. Kirk had nothing to offer Jamie, and Jamie would likely bring a heap of other issues to Kirk's peaceful life.

Just let it go, man. He's got a job, he's got some contacts, and he's smart. He'll be fine.

But as Kirk turned to head into the living room, he stopped because his brain was already thinking about the next time he could make it to the restaurant to check up on Jamie.

KIRK FOUGHT THE URGE TO THROTTLE JAMIE AS THE KID FLIRTED mercilessly with the debonair older man sitting at the counter. Jamie had caught Kirk's eye more than once and each time the men made eye contact Jamie upped the flirtatious smiles and laughter with the creep.

Kirk supposed it was unfair to assume the old guy was a creep just because of his fifty-some years and the fact that Jamie was going so over-the-top with the flirting and the man was practically salivating on the counter he was eating up the attention so much.

But Kirk knew the man. And creep was putting it nicely.

Several of the young gay men at the teen center had mentioned Donald Carter's name in reference to salacious comments and unwanted advances. And good ol' Don had been tried in the disappearance of a gay teen a couple years back. Kirk's gut told him Don had something to do with the missing kid, but the department had pursued multiple suspects and Carter's lawyer got him off on reasonable doubt.

Donald had been a thorn in Kirk's side ever since. Obviously born and bred on "old money," Don Carter was rich by many standards. He'd have his driver cruise by the teen center at least once a week. Monthly, Donald's car would wait outside the center while—bless his generous soul—he would dally in the center eye-fucking the young men while under the pretense of making a sizable donation.

Kirk or other officers had been present several times during

Carter's visits. The man was doing nothing illegal, was giving large sums of money to a very deserving cause, and didn't make a scene. The police had no official reason to keep Don away. The center had a delicate balancing act of keeping a very benevolent donor happy while still protecting the young folk who frequented the establishment.

"You know who that is, right?" Sam spoke sharply from Kirk's side before pulling up a seat.

"Yep." Kirk sighed. "Unfortunately."

"Donald Carter is scum. Creepy, abusive, scary, and predatory scum." Sam gritted his teeth. "What the hell is Jamie doing being so friendly?"

"You know as well as I do that Donny Boy is as charismatic as they come. Wines them, dines them, and promises them the moon and stars." Kirk's eyes barely left Jamie for more than a split second as he spoke with Sam.

"I still can't believe he got off on that kid's disappearance. Everyone knew he was at least involved somehow." Sam shook his head. "It's disgusting."

Kirk nodded. "One of the biggest screw-ups and disappointments of all the court cases I've ever witnessed."

"You think Jamie likes him?" Sam screwed up his nose.

"I don't know." Kirk ran a hand through his hair. "I think the kid is trying to make me jealous."

"Is it working?"

"Doesn't matter. I wouldn't want anyone getting involved with Don Carter." Kirk's angry words rumbled through his chest.

"But you do like Jamie?" Sam prodded.

Kirk rolled his eyes. "He's cute. But we're definitely on different pages with where we are in life and what we want."

"Different doesn't have to be bad."

"True. Differences aren't bad, but the kid seems determined to butt heads with me."

"Think about it from his point of view." Sam shifted in his

chair. "He's a young gay kid, outed without his consent, college ripped away, parents disown him, and his father gives him a beat down on the front lawn." Sam frowned. "And then you show up to diffuse the situation and rescue him. You've seen him at the lowest point in his life. He's human and wants to make up for that night. Convince you he's stronger than that, show you he doesn't *need* you or anything else, prove to the world he can make it on his own. But deep down, he's scared to death, lonely, and has no idea how he's going to overcome the big fuck-you he was just handed."

Kirk took a deep breath. "You're right. It's just frustrating that I'm able and willing to help him, but he won't accept it."

"You offered your assistance?"

"Yeah, laundry, food, shower, bed. His own bed." Kirk wrinkled his forehead. "He took the shower and food and did his laundry. Before I could talk him into at least a night or two in a nice bed he found Bethany's underwear and flipped the fuck out."

"Bethany, your wife?" Sam's eyes widened.

"Ex-wife. We've been divorced a while. She's moving out, but...it's complicated." Kirk grimaced.

"Well, I'm sure Jamie latched onto you being married as one more reason to hate you and want nothing to do with you." Sam slapped Kirk on the shoulder. "I'll put a bug in his ear that Don is bad news. Maybe coming from me it will sink in a little better."

"Thanks," Kirk mumbled. "Sure as shit isn't going to listen to me."

Jamie took that moment to saunter over to the table.

"Sam." He nodded at Kirk's former colleague. "Officer Pathetic Stalker. You gentlemen need anything else or are you ready to leave?" Jamie smiled and batted his lashes.

"I'm heading out. We were just talking about your Baby Boomer Creeper up there." Sam lifted his chin to indicate Don.

"The man is harmless. He's eating and getting his flirt on. No different than Officer Kirk stalking me at my place of employment multiple times a week." Jamie pulled Kirk's ticket from his apron. "You can pay up front, sir."

As Jamie turned to leave, Kirk spoke up. "Wait. Seriously, take our word for it. Don Carter isn't a very nice guy."

"Green isn't a good color on you, Officer. He's charming, well-educated, sophisticated, and interested in getting to know me rather than mothering me." Jamie shrugged. "Sorry, find another charity boy to take care of. I'm moving on to bigger and better."

Sam and Kirk watched as Jamie stomped off.

"Fuck," Kirk grumbled.

"The stubbornness is strong in that one." Sam shook his head. "Problem is he's going to get himself in a heap of trouble trying to prove to you *and* himself how much he doesn't need or want *you*. Don will step right in and scoop him up. Jamie will have no clue what hit him."

"I *know* all this, Stein." Kirk worked to keep his voice at an acceptable level. "The question is what do I *do* about it?"

"Keep an eye on Jamie and a closer eye on Don." Sam lifted a shoulder. "Make sure the teen center knows to watch out for suspicious activity. Give Jamie your contact info. But aside from that, if no laws are broken, you're going to have to let Jamie take care of himself. Sooner or later, he'll wise up."

"Or get himself hurt in the process." Kirk had a sinking feeling all aspects of his life would take a chaotic turn in the very near future.

5

"Thanks for meeting me," Bethany chirped as she sipped her drink. "This place is nice. When Brandon suggested it, I worried it would be a real dive. I mean, it's not as upscale as Sparks or somewhere like that, but I like the atmosphere."

Kirk nodded and sipped his beer. "So, where *is* Brandon? He's not making a great first impression if he's standing you up."

Bethany cocked her head and smiled. "Relax. He still has five minutes before he's even close to being late." She fiddled with the salt shaker. "I really want you to like him. He's a great guy. And he's not like a rebound or something. I purposely took it slow and didn't dive head first into anything."

"I'm sure I'll like him just fine." Kirk winked.

"He's got a few gay friends."

Kirk chuckled. "And just like that his gay friends and I may know each other and just have to hit it off and hook up and fall in love and it will be perfect, right?"

Bethany blushed. "Okay, hearing you say it *that* way sounds stupid." She glanced at her cellphone's screen. "I'm just saying, if we ever want to go on a double date or something, Brandon could probably provide a guy."

"Gee, thanks. That doesn't make me sound desperate and incapable of finding my own date at all." Kirk wrinkled his nose. "Better yet, it doesn't make Brandon sound anything like a pimp."

"I'm a pimp now?" An amused voice sounded behind Kirk.

Bethany hopped from her seat and hugged the man. "No, I said you have gay friends."

"And that you could *provide a guy* for me if we ever wanted to double date." Kirk laughed and shook Brandon's hand. "I'm Kirk, nice to meet you."

"Yeah, *provide a guy* doesn't exactly sound on the up and up." Brandon kept Bethany at his side and returned Kirk's handshake. "Good to finally meet you."

Over the next half hour, Kirk relaxed as drinks were refilled, food was served, and small talk flowed nicely.

And then his evening took a turn for the worse.

Jamie sauntered into the bar looking pleased as punch to be there. And delectable. And adorable. And sexy as hell.

"Who's that?" Bethany's gaze followed Kirk's.

"An underage punk who isn't even supposed to be *in* a bar." Kirk watched in bubbling frustration as Jamie leaned against the counter and caught the bartender's eye. "Let alone ordering alcohol," Kirk grumbled.

"He's cute." Bethany chomped on a fry.

"He's a pain in the ass."

"How do you know him?" Brandon winked at Bethany, but Kirk was too busy staring at Jamie to care. "Long story. Not really mine to tell." Kirk took a few more bites of his burger, washed it all down with a swig of beer, and pulled out his wallet. "But I need to get him out of here."

"Wait." Bethany reached for his arm. "You're leaving? Just because some underage kid snuck into a bar?"

Kirk squeezed her hand on his arm. "It's more than that. He can't afford to get in trouble. He needs his job."

"If he got in then his fake ID must be pretty good. Not a huge chance he's gonna get caught," Brandon chimed in.

"They aren't scanning cards." Kirk shook his head. "He must have slipped by somehow. I'm going to talk to him and make sure he leaves. Then I'll talk to the manager to be sure he doesn't get back in."

Kirk tossed down two twenties. "If I'm not back when you decide to head out, I hope you have a great evening." He shook Brandon's hand. "Nice meeting you. Treat her right. She's great and deserves only the best." Kirk turned to Bethany and pulled her from her seat to gather her into a hug. "You did good, Bethy. Take care and be happy." He kissed her cheek before turning toward the bar.

Jamie's wide eyes belied his bravado and confidence the moment he saw Kirk barreling toward the bar. The kid downed the drink in front of him and signaled the bartender for one more before Kirk could weave his way through the crowd. By the time Kirk wedged his body behind Jamie's—as if he only planned to order a drink, Jamie had slurped down the second drink.

"You're going to stop drinking like a damn underage punk ass fish, toss your money on the counter, and follow me out of here right now." Kirk's words were low and threatening in Jamie's ear.

Jamie tossed a glance over his shoulder. "And if I don't?"

"If you don't, you'll end up in trouble and losing that job you claim to need so badly." Kirk put a firm hand on the kid's elbow. "Not to mention...a record for underage drinking won't help with the college prospects."

Jamie's shoulders slumped and his chin dropped to his chest. He drained his glass before he pushed it away and fished in his pocket for money. Before he could find what he was looking for, Kirk tossed a twenty on the bar and nudged Jamie.

"Follow me. We're going out the side door. Keep your head

down. We don't need anyone recognizing you or questioning your age." Kirk headed toward the side door with Jamie close behind. Once they exited the building, Kirk turned toward the parking lot. "I'll give you a ride wherever you're going."

Jamie's shoulders still slumped as he shuffled to Kirk's car. Kirk popped the locks and climbed in. "Where ya headed?" Kirk asked as he fiddled with the heater.

Jamie's words were muffled.

"Where?"

"I said I don't have anywhere to go tonight!" Jamie shoved a hand through his hair and glared out the window.

Kirk's mood matched Jamie's throughout the entire drive to his townhouse— brooding and silent.

Jamie's silence was broken when Kirk pulled into his driveway. "What are we doing here? Is your *wife* home?"

"Actually, I was meeting my *ex-wife* and her new *boyfriend* for dinner and drinks when I saw some underage punk ass kid in a bar drinking. *Illegally*. So, no, Bethany isn't here. She'll be taking the rest of her stuff over the next week or so. You can shower and sleep here, at least for tonight."

Jamie's chin jutted out and he looked like he was about to argue, but then he closed his eyes and sighed. "Thanks. It's cold as fuck out there, and I didn't really know where I was going to stay."

"What the hell were you thinking going into a bar?" Kirk turned in his seat to face Jamie.

"That a little alcohol would warm me up and maybe I could think of a place to stay." Jamie shrugged. "I mean, I may have something worked out for a more permanent place, but I gotta think it over and be sure it's going to work."

Kirk sighed heavily. "Just *please* tell me it has nothing to do with Donald Carter."

"Not that it's any of your business, but what do you have against the guy? He's charming and lonely. Not to mention rich and generous. If I did have something to do with him what would be so terrible about it?" Jamie crossed his arms over his chest.

Kirk rubbed a hand over his face. "Oh hell, I don't know, maybe the fact that he was a prime suspect in a young male's disappearance not too many years ago. Or the fact that he eye-fucks every kid he sees at the teen center, *especially* the guys. And maybe the fact that a lot of the boys at the teen center say Don is a total creeper. Is that enough for you?"

Jamie rolled his eyes. "A prime suspect? But not convicted? Well, then he must have been innocent."

"He wasn't *innocent*. He knew, he *knows*, something about that kid. But he had a good attorney." Kirk shut off the car and threw open his door.

Jamie followed.

Once inside the house, Jamie continued. "So, no convictions, no real complaints, you just don't like him because he's old, gay, and rich? Me thinks you're just jealous, Officer Envious."

"I'm jealous of Don Carter?"

"I mean, he's openly gay, he's rich, and he's powerful. What's not to envy?" Jamie cocked his head. "He's basically everything you're not."

Kirk turned on his heel and headed toward the kitchen. "I don't envy creepy pedophiles who use their money and power to bully their way through life." Kirk tossed his keys on the counter.

"Whatever you say." Jamie shrugged.

"So are you planning to stay at his place?" Kirk pinned Jamie with a stare.

"Again, none of your business. I'm working on some things." Jamie's eyes wandered to the fridge. "You got anything to eat?"

Kirk sighed, but his need to shelter and protect the kid won out over his curiosity. "Yeah, help yourself. I'm going to shower. You can shower whenever you want. Guestroom has sheets laid out, just make the bed. Or sleep on the couch if you're more comfortable there." Kirk stalked from the room leaving Jamie alone in the kitchen.

Jamie leaned against the counter and held his head in his hands. Why did Kirk have to be so beautiful and caring and annoying? Why couldn't Jamie just accept his hospitality and take things one day at a time? But everything about letting Kirk take care of him made Jamie feel helpless, desperate, and pathetic.

*You **are** desperate, dumbass.*

"Yeah, but he doesn't need to know that," Jamie muttered.

Jamie had let one man cower him, hurt him, and make him weak. He had no plans of letting Officer Kirkland take over where his father had left off.

Do you really think Kirk would do any of those things?

Jamie shook his head.

Then maybe you should swallow your pride and admit you could use his help.

"No way, I don't *need* him." Jamie pushed from the counter. "I'll figure something out on my own." He opened the fridge. His stomach rumbled happily as he pulled out a pot of leftover spaghetti.

Kirk wiped off the steamy mirror before wrapping the towel around his waist. While the hot shower had felt wonderful, it had done very little to ease his frustrations regarding Jamie. The kid was stubborn and prickly.

And young.

So damn young.

But Kirk admitted to himself that he'd thought of little else since the night he pulled up to Jamie's home to find the kid being beaten to a pulp. What kind of father did that to his own child? And Jamie's mother had stood by and watched, wringing her hands as if the beating was necessary to cure her evil son.

Jamie hadn't wanted to press charges even though the police had encouraged it, as well as the attending staff at the hospital. But the kid had refused with very few words of explanation. Kirk had filed a report of the incident, but beyond that he could do little else except make sure Jamie's dad didn't seek out his son to finish the job.

Maybe that was why Kirk felt so drawn to Jamie. Perhaps Kirk simply wanted to assure the kid was safe from his father.

Lots of the kids at the center have shitty fathers. You aren't hung up on them.

More than likely it was Don Carter's interest in Jamie that kept the kid on his mind.

Don Carter has been a creep and predator long before Jamie. You never took a personal interest in protecting any of his other targets.

Jamie's beautiful gray-green eyes, that tiny smirky smile, and the soft curve of his ass echoed in Kirk's mind. The kid was damn gorgeous and had an intriguing personality to boot. *That* was the most likely reason Jamie was on Kirk's mind twenty-four seven.

Acknowledgement is the first step to solving any problem.

"Shut up," Kirk muttered as he stared at the reflection in the mirror. Twenty-nine, gay, divorced. "Fuck, I'm a mess."

Maybe Jamie is just what you need to help your mess make sense.

"Shut *up*," Kirk growled again. He ran the towel through his hair before pulling on a pair of light gray sweats.

Kirk wandered to the kitchen to check on Jamie, but found an empty room smelling slightly of spaghetti and a lone plate and fork in the sink. Kirk glanced toward the living room, but no Jamie. Heading to the guestroom, expecting to find Jamie making the bed or in the shower, Kirk was shocked to see the kid sprawled out on the bed in just a t-shirt and shorts. Jamie's short hair was damp and a towel was spread over the back of the door. Only the light from the hall lit the room.

Kirk's heart clenched at the sight. Jamie was beautiful, period. But asleep, he looked younger and more innocent than Kirk had ever seen. Strength, determination, and courage also radiated from Jamie in stark contrast to his soft innocence.

Kirk assumed Jamie hadn't taken time to make the bed. It looked as if the kid had showered and fallen straight asleep before his head barely hit the pillow. Kirk pulled the blanket from the end of the bed and gently spread it over Jamie before quietly exiting the room.

Several minutes later, as he lay in bed down the hall from

Jamie, he tossed and turned as sleep teased the edge of his mind. Right at the moment Kirk was about to give in to slumber, he felt his body jerk awake. What had he heard? Was it Jamie?

Kirk's ears roared as he listened, trying to decide if the noise that had awakened him was Jamie or not. When the kid's muffled yell sounded down the hallway, Kirk bounded from bed and rushed to the guestroom.

Flipping on the light to find Jamie curled in a tight ball, clutching his stomach, groaning and sobbing was much too reminiscent of the first night Kirk had met the young man.

"Jamie," Kirk whispered and touched Jamie's arm gently. "Jamie, it's Kirk. You're just dreaming. Jamie?"

Jamie's eyes shot open and he popped up in bed looking around wildly.

"Jamie? It's me, Kirk. You're in the guestroom at my place. You were having a nightmare." Kirk walked the short distance to the bathroom to turn on the light before switching off the overhead bedroom light so it wasn't so bright. "You want some water?"

Jamie's answer was a single nod in the dim shadows.

By the time Kirk returned, Jamie had likely been to the restroom if the room's darkness was any evidence to go by.

"Sorry about that," Jamie mumbled from under the covers, his voice soft and tinged with shame.

"Nothing to be sorry about." Kirk walked to the edge of the bed and sat down knowing he was likely pushing his luck. He held out the water as a peace offering.

Jamie shifted, his face catching just the edge of the light filtering in through the window. "Thanks." He sat up a bit, and Kirk leaned his back against the headboard.

"You have the nightmares a lot?"

"Never before," Jamie huffed.

"So only since your dad?"

"No, never. Tonight's the first time I've ever had one."

Kirk frowned and studied Jamie. "Why do you think that is?"

Jamie shook his head.

"I'm sorry it happened here. If I did anything to make you uncomfortable or put you in a fearful position, I apologize." Kirk's heart squeezed tight in his chest.

"No, it wasn't you. I mean, you *are* a creeper, but you didn't do anything." Jamie smirked and took another drink. "Honestly, I was sleeping better than I have since that night. Can't dream much when you're scared, cold, and uncomfortable. A bed, blanket and pillow gave me the comfort to fall into a deep sleep. Probably why the dream came."

"Makes sense." Kirk nodded. "What was it about?" Kirk asked the question even though he knew the answer. Jamie's psyche had been reliving that night of terror, pain, and humiliation.

Jamie rubbed a hand over his face and sniffed before tossing the water bottle to the ground. "My dad. Throwing me out, screaming at me, kicking me, hating me."

Kirk remained silent as the words filled the room.

"But...in the dream, you never came. The scene just kept playing over and over and every time I'd think someone was coming to help, that *you* were coming to help, it would stop and start on replay with no one ever coming to stop it." Jamie's breath shuddered from his chest. "He just never stopped and you never came." Jamie's words were thick with emotion as he fell to the side on his pillow.

Kirk watched Jamie for a few moments. "I'm here now, and I'll always come for you."

～

JAMIE WOKE IN A COCOON OF WARM, DELICIOUS MAN ARMS AND blanket.

His eyes cracked open, reluctant to interrupt the beautiful sleep he'd been enjoying.

In the shadowy morning light Jamie recalled the guestroom at Kirk's, the shower, the bed. And the nightmare.

Kirk coming to help him.

And now Kirk holding him against his chest in a fiercely protective embrace.

Jamie entertained the idea of breaking free, of being angry, of storming from Kirk's house. But the thoughts were there and gone within seconds.

Jamie had never felt so helpless, alone, and scared as he did in the nightmare. Kirk hadn't come to him in his dream. But Kirk was there now. And Jamie felt safe, warm, and so very sleepy. He closed his eyes and nuzzled his nose against Kirk's chest.

KIRK DEBATED WAKING JAMIE OR CONTINUING TO HOLD THE YOUNG man and savoring the most enjoyable wake-up he'd ever had. Kirk had been aware when Jamie woke earlier. Having Jamie snuggle deeply into Kirk's embrace had been heavenly and Kirk didn't want it to end.

"So I guess you finally wore me down and got me in bed, creeper." Jamie's voice rumbled against Kirk's chest.

Kirk kept his arms around Jamie and chuckled. "You figured me out. I had to play that nightmare just right to make sure I'd end up here."

Kirk felt Jamie's smile.

"Well, now that you have me here, what are your intentions, Officer Pervy Pants?" Jamie's sleepy gaze tipped up to meet Kirk's.

Kirk bent his head and rested his forehead against Jamie's. "Contrary to your suspicions, I actually had no plans of getting you in bed. Hopes, dreams, and wishes? Yes. But no hard and fast plans. So, I don't have a damn clue what to do with you now that you're here."

Jamie's teeth pulled at his bottom lip as his pupils dilated with desire. "You could kiss me." "Will you knee me in the nuts if I do?" Kirk nuzzled his nose along Jamie's cheek.

"That move is reserved for unwanted advances."

"I thought anything to do with me was unwanted." Kirk's mouth was only a breath away from Jamie's.

"Maybe I've reevaluated my position on your advances," Jamie whispered.

"Yeah?" Kirk feathered his lips at the corner of Jamie's.

"Yeah." Jamie moaned and tipped his head back allowing Kirk access to his chin and neck. "Definitely wanted."

Kirk groaned and gave in to the desire to feast upon Jamie's skin. Kirk trailed his mouth along Jamie's jawline, down his neck, dipping his tongue in the hollow at the other man's throat, before gripping the back of Jamie's head and hovering just above his mouth.

His heart pounded a rhythm between their bodies. Tension and desire hung thick in the air. Anticipation lay heavy.

Just a kiss.

Nothing more.

Just a kiss.

Between two men wildly attracted to each other and drawn together beyond reason.

Just a kiss.

Between two men with very little in common. Two men at very different places in life. Two men who likely needed the entanglement like they needed an extra hole in their heads.

Kirk inched his mouth closer, hesitating only a moment as he watched Jamie's eyes flutter shut. As their lips met and red-hot electricity flowed between them, Kirk knew immediately that nothing with Jamie would ever be *just a kiss*.

Lips caressed, tongues explored, hard bodies pressed together allowing passion and friction to build a dangerous and exciting heat as his arms tightened and his hands grasped and held Jamie tight.

Jamie's mouth was the sweetest Kirk had ever tasted and everything he'd always felt was missing from his life seemed to burst forth.

Nothing had ever felt as right as this moment.

Breaking apart for a breath, Kirk's gaze met Jamie's and clung as tightly as their bodies.

"Whoa."

"Yeah, we definitely have to make more time for that." Kirk stroked the back of Jamie's head.

Jamie's eyes widened. "Shit. The time. What time is it?" He vaulted from the bed and grabbed his phone. "Nooo, I'm going to be so late." Jamie rushed around the room gathering his meager belongings.

"Hey, it's okay." Kirk stood and stretched. "I'll give you a ride. I'll grab us some breakfast while you wash up and then meet you at the backdoor. You'll make it."

Fifteen minutes later, Jamie barreled down the hallway toward the utility room and caught the bottle of water Kirk tossed his way. "Thanks, man."

"No problem," Kirk quipped as they descended the stairs and climbed in the car.

"I mean, for the water, the ride, everything." Jamie's cheeks heated with the blush.

"Again, no problem." Kirk pulled the car onto the street. "Listen, I'm on a wicked shift run the next five days. If I have time, and I'm in the area, I'll pop in, but no guarantees. You're welcome to stay at my place even if I'm not there."

Jamie was already shaking his head. "No, that doesn't feel right. I can't be waking up in your bed, in your arms, kissing you like that and still expect to keep my head on straight. After this morning, all I want to do is move in and have every wake-up be just like today."

"Fine by me," Kirk teased. "Seriously, I'm all for it."

"No, we can't do that. We'd be putting too much pressure on

us to work if I was living there." Jamie shook his head again. "We need to do this the normal way. Cohabitating after one kiss with all the mess we both know is between us would set us up for failure."

"So, what do we do?"

"How 'bout we date? See each other when we can, build up the anticipation of our next time together, and get to know each other outside of police officer and victim?" Jamie's words held uncertainty and hope.

"How'd we go from you despising me to dating?" Kirk raised a brow.

Jamie shrugged. "Maybe I never really despised you. I just don't want you thinking I'm that weak, pathetic kid you found on the sidewalk."

"Never thought that. Ever."

"I'll keep that in mind." Jamie blushed.

"Okay, I'm good with that." Kirk smiled. "But where are you going to stay? I can't go to work and be worried about where you're staying."

"Let me talk to some friends at the center after work and see what I can work out." Jamie rubbed his palms on his pants.

"What if you can't work something out?"

"I'll let you know if I can't, and we can figure it out from there?" Jamie raised his brow in question.

"Okay, but there's only one problem with that answer."

"What's that?"

"You don't know my number." Kirk smiled and pulled his phone from his jacket. "Here, put in your number and then text yourself."

Jamie grinned. "Good idea." He inputted the numbers and saved them just as Kirk pulled up outside the restaurant.

"See? Right on time." Kirk put the car in Park.

Jamie gathered his bag. "Thank you. So much. For the ride

and, well, you know. Everything." He sprung from the car and jogged toward the door.

One kiss.

One kiss had changed so much.

Nothing was completely solved. Some issues were still up in the air. But Kirk couldn't stop the smile that teased at his lips as he watched that prickly kid disappear behind the door.

7

Five long hellish days.

Kirk had barely slept.

Lost a victim to a gunshot wound.

Had a call to a repeat domestic abuse situation.

And found a kid dead from an overdose.

Five days spent dealing with what felt like the worst society had to offer.

Five days questioning his career choice and wondering if he ever really made a difference.

And he hadn't been able to see Jamie even once.

They'd texted a little.

Jamie assured him he was safe. One of the managers at the restaurant needed a house-sitter for a few days and had asked if Jamie was interested. The house was within walking-distance to the restaurant, required Jamie to water the plants, feed some fish, and make sure the trash was out on the right day along with collecting the mail. The best part was it provided a couch to sleep on.

Kirk had a strong suspicion the house-sitting gig could have been done without Jamie sleeping on the couch, but he appreciated the manager giving Jamie a place to stay. Kirk wondered if one of the Breakfast Club guys had let the manager know of Jamie's situation.

Now Kirk glanced at his phone when it buzzed with an incoming text from Jamie.

CAN YOU MEET ME AT THE CENTER RATHER THAN THE RESTAURANT?

SURE. KIRK THUMBED THE RESPONSE.

GREAT, GOT SOMETHING I NEED TO TELL YOU.

WHAT? KIRK'S EYES IMMEDIATELY NARROWED.

I'LL TELL YOU WHEN I SEE YOU. JUST HAVE AN OPEN MIND AND DON'T *get pissed.*

KIRK CLOSED HIS EYES AND SIGHED. HE WAS EXHAUSTED COMING off his fifth overnight shift. Kirk didn't like surprises, and he didn't like feeling out of the loop. What the hell had the kid been up to?

He quickly typed in his response. *Yeah, that makes me feel all warm and fuzzy.*

JAMIE SENT A WINKY SMILEY FACE. IT'S NOT BAD. IT'S A GOOD THING.

. . .

"Mmhm," Kirk mumbled and turned his car toward the teen center.

Kirk's stomach plummeted the moment he pulled up to the center and saw Don Carter's driver leaning against the dark sedan.

"Oh, hell, no." Kirk vaulted from the car and made a beeline for the center just as Jamie walked out the door. Kirk grabbed his arm and led him back inside. "We need to talk."

"You can't be mad. This is going to work out just great." Jamie pointed to a study room where the two could talk privately.

"Anything that has to do with Donald Carter will never work out great unless your plan is to end up raped and or dead." Kirk gestured toward the window where Don's car could be seen.

"Just hear me out, and listen to the plan." Jamie pouted and edged closer to Kirk. "Hi," he whispered and gazed up longingly.

Kirk sighed and pulled the kid into his arms. Kissing the side of his head, and hugging him close before tipping Jamie's chin and kissing him softly. "Hi," he whispered gruffly back. "Missed you."

"Missed you, too." Jamie bit his lip.

"And now you're going to tell me that I'm losing you to Don Carter? Not the way I pictured my five days of work ending. Thought we'd spend some time together." Kirk rubbed the back of his neck, tension and worry building.

Jamie sat at the table. "So, Don offered to let me stay with him."

Kirk's eyes bugged from his head. "*I* offered to let you stay with *me*."

"That's different."

"How?"

"Don hasn't seen me at my worst. Don didn't rescue me from

the most humiliating moment of my life." Jamie tapped his fingers on the table.

"I don't see you that way. I told you that." Kirk flopped down at the table across from Jamie.

"And I'm not hoping to date Don and get to know him better." Jamie's words were soft.

Kirk smiled slightly. "While I love hearing that, can't you work out something, *anything*, better than walking right into the arms of a complete and total creep?"

"Listen, Don isn't all that bad." Jamie held up his hand to fend off Kirk's argument. "Just listen. He lost a grandson a few years ago. Really tore him up. He knows I'm trying to work and get back into school. All I have to do is help out around the house, go to basketball games and movies with him, and go out to eat with him a few nights a week."

"Yeah, I'm sure that's *all*," Kirk huffed and rolled his eyes.

"He looks at me as a grandson, that's it. I'll be like the grandson he lost."

"And what do you get from this fantastic little set up?"

"Aside from room and board, Don wants to use the money he saved for his grandson's education to help me out with college." Jamie's eyes were bright with hope and excitement. "How awesome is that?"

Kirk stared, open-mouthed at the kid for several moments trying to gather the thoughts in his sleep-deprived mind. Finally, he croaked out, "Are you fucking serious right now?"

Jamie's face fell. "Yeah, I'm dead serious. This is my way out. Spend time with a nice old guy, help him out, and he gets me back on my feet and into college. I'd be stupid to turn this down. Why can't you see this is a good thing?"

Kirk gritted his teeth to keep from screaming. "Why can't *you* see that Don is playing you like a damn fiddle?"

"You've always been jealous of anything having to do with him." Jamie jutted his chin and crossed his arms.

"I'm not jealous, damn it, I'm concerned. He's *not* a good guy, Jamie. He's dangerous. Doesn't it seem weird to you that he'd just offer all of this with no strings attached?" Kirk stood and paced the room.

"I'll be doing my part. He's a lonely old man, and he lost a grandson he loved very much. Why can't you see that this will be good for both Don and me?" Jamie stood and walked toward Kirk. "It's not him against you. He's like a kind old neighbor guy I want to help and be nice to."

"What am I?" Kirk frowned.

"You," Jamie whispered as he hooked his arms around Kirk's neck, "are the sexy older cop who I very much want to get to know and do all sorts of dirty things with."

"As great as that sounds, I need you to promise me you'll stay in touch, and when you realize Don is as bad, if not worse, than I've been telling you then you'll get out of there." Kirk held Jamie by the shoulders.

"He's not," Jamie started but stopped when Kirk shook him gently.

"Just promise me you'll admit you're wrong and let me help you when this terrible fucking joke of a plan goes south." Kirk's anger and exhaustion mixed with his worry for Jamie.

"I'm grown. I think I can make my own damn decisions. Why can't you just see me as an equal and not as some kid who needs his hand held and his nose wiped?" Jamie jerked away from Kirk's hold. "At least Don is treating me like an adult and showing me some respect which is more than I can say for you. Maybe you should promise me you'll admit when *you're* wrong and offer an apology when you realize Don may be a bit eccentric, but is just a lonely old guy who doesn't mean anyone any harm."

Kirk shook his head. "Whatever."

"Is everything okay here, Jamie?" A voice sounded from the doorway.

Kirk whipped around to find Don standing there. He gritted his teeth and swallowed the acid that boiled up from his belly. Kirk stepped forward and jabbed a finger at Don. "Carter, I'm watching you. One hair on this kid's head gets harmed and I'll drag you to the station so fast you won't know what happened."

"Officer Kirkland, so nice to see you. I'd like to thank you for your continued service to the city of New York. Shame we haven't seen much of each other since that terrible debacle at the courthouse." Don sauntered into the room and stood next to Jamie. "And Jamie is in no danger at my house. He will be well taken care of and will find his own worth in knowing he's bringing joy and pleasure to a crotchety old man." Don turned toward Jamie. "We should head out. We have dinner reservations."

Jamie nodded. "I'll be right out."

Kirk and Jamie watched Don retreat from the room.

"Jamie, please, I don't trust him."

"Then trust me and my judgement. This is a good opportunity, and I need to take it." Jamie squared his shoulders. "I hope you'll stand beside me. I'd very much like to continue whatever this is we've started."

Kirk stared at Jamie for several moments. "I don't know. I just don't know."

Jamie sighed heavily. "You have my number."

"And you have mine."

"Do you want me to use it?" Jamie countered.

"I guess we'll see." Kirk frowned and turned to leave. As he walked past Don, the feeling of dread grew in his stomach and his chest clenched. Don's smarmy smile all but proved Kirk's bad feeling. But what was he to do? Jamie was a grown-up by law. Kirk had no control over him. Kirk had no options other than to let Jamie make his own mistakes and pray he stayed alive and well long enough to learn from them.

Kirk sat in his car and watched with sick anger and concern

as Jamie threw his bag in the trunk of Don's car and climbed into the backseat with the old man.

Kirk wasn't much of a praying man, but he said a silent prayer that he hadn't just witnessed Jamie walk right into the fox's den.

8

"So, that's the grand tour." Don spoke from the door of Jamie's new room. "I expect you to keep your room neat and tidy and clean up after yourself in the kitchen and bathroom, but I, of course, have a housekeeper to do the majority of the cleaning. Aside from the basement and my office, the entire house is open, and I invite you to make yourself at home." Don's posture suggested he wasn't keen on chitchat and was ready to go. "We do have reservations so we should get going."

"Let me just text Kirk." Jamie held up his phone after tossing his bag on the bed. "Then I'll be ready to go."

I'M HERE. MY ROOM IS ON THE FARTHEST END OF THE HOUSE AWAY FROM Don's. No worries. Heading to dinner now. Will text later if not too late. This house is ah-maz-ing!

JAMIE STUFFED HIS PHONE IN HIS POCKET AND FOLLOWED DON down the hall.

"The officer has you on a tight leash, huh?" Don paused at the door to the garage where Cliff, the driver, had the car waiting.

"Huh?" Jamie frowned. "Kirk? Nah, he just worries. We just started seeing each other so it's all pretty new. Feeling things out, ya know?"

"Well, I hope he understands that you have certain responsibilities here now. You aren't at his beck and call." Don raised a brow and waited.

"Never was at his beck and call. He's not my father or my keeper. No worries." Jamie jutted his chin.

"That's what I like to hear." Don reached out and chucked Jamie's chin.

The two men climbed into the car.

Jamie's phone buzzed and he pulled it from his pocket.

NEVER TOO LATE. TEXT AT ANY TIME. BE SAFE.

JAMIE STARTED TO UNLOCK THE SCREEN AND REPLY, BUT DON cleared his throat and gave him a pointed look. Jamie blushed and slid the phone back into his pocket.

"That's better." Don nodded. "I don't care for my companions to be more interested in their phone and friends than me."

Jamie's blood quivered in his veins. He squirmed in his seat. "So, um, tell me about your family."

"I'm an only child. Never married. My parents died several years ago." Don shrugged. "As far as family goes, I'm completely alone. But I feel my life is full in terms of friends and wealth and power." The older man puffed out his chest. "I have *a lot* of influence in many areas. You and everyone who knows me are lucky to keep me on their good side."

Jamie's heart pounded. Where was the kind and charming old man from the restaurant who smiled over extra cream and sugar in his coffee? Wait, *only child*? *Never married*? "Um, what about your grandson? You said you had a grandson." Jamie struggled to keep his words steady. A very reasonable explanation had to exist for everything.

Had to.

"Did I say grandson?" Don wrinkled his brow and chuckled. "Getting old is such a bother. I likely meant to say Alec was *like* a grandson to me. Such a good boy. You remind me a lot of him."

Jamie's head set to spinning upon comprehending what the words meant. "So, you lied to me?" He'd been in Don's presence less than half a day. How could everything be spiraling so quickly?

"Dear boy, a slip of words is an innocent mistake. I miss Alec with all of my heart every single day. You remind me so much of him. I likely was just showing my age and senility when I called him my grandson." Don reached over and stroked Jamie's leg.

"I remind you of him? In a grandson way or in a lover and companion way? Which was he?" Jamie flinched and moved his leg from the touch.

"In every single way that is important. What Alec and I had transcended relationship norms. We were above labels and roles. We shared an all-encompassing love." Don's hand found Jamie's leg again and gripped heavily.

"What happened to him? To Alec?" Jamie shifted so Don's hand was more on his knee.

"Alec struggled with anxiety and depression. He had his own demons. No matter the therapy or the medication or the love I tried to show, none of it was enough." Don closed his eyes and sighed.

"What happened to him?" Jamie persisted.

"My poor boy left a suicide note and disappeared. His body has never been found. He vanished." A tear glittered at the corner of Don's eye.

"So you don't *know* if he's dead? Maybe he just left? Wanted to be on his own?" *Because he realized what a psycho you are.* Jamie's mind flooded with fear and confusion. What the hell had he gotten himself into?

Kirk had been right.

So very right.

Fuck.

Kirk.

Jamie needed to contact Kirk.

"Alec loved me as much as I loved him. Our hearts were one. He never would have left me. My soul felt his loss. Our love was strong, but his demons were stronger." Don wiped the tear from his eye. "Ah, here we are. I think you'll just *adore* this place. Some of the best food and wine in all of New York."

"Pretty sure they don't let nineteen year olds drink wine at most restaurants." Jamie reached for his phone.

"Nonsense, you will need to learn that you can do *anything* now that you're with me. It's a privilege that comes with my power." Don's gaze pinned Jamie. "Leave your phone. It's not needed."

"I feel better keeping it with me." Jamie attempted nonchalance.

"And I feel better knowing my companion can follow directions. I'll need you present and attentive during dinner. I can't look like I have a simple teenage beauty on my arm, now can I?" Don gripped Jamie's wrist. "Leave it here. Cliff will keep it safe."

Jamie's breath came in quick puffs, his nostrils flared, and his mind ran through scenarios of what he could and should do.

Refuse to leave the phone.

Kick Don and flee.

Call 911.

Call Kirk.

But his panicked mind froze with the overwhelming realization that he'd been lied to, tricked, suckered, and was now stuck between a rock and a hard place. Jamie placed the phone on the car seat.

New plan.

Follow along.

Keep Don happy for the time being.

Contact Kirk and get the hell away from Don Carter as soon as humanly possible.

Jamie smiled slightly. "Sure, no problem. I can eat a meal without being glued to my phone screen. It's not like I'm some dumb kid. I'm looking forward to meeting your friends. Maybe you can teach me about wine."

"That's what I like to hear. Good boy." Don nodded and slid his hand from Jamie's wrist to hold his hand. "One thing you'll learn, it's always easier to just let me have my way. Things can get so messy and ugly if not."

Jamie took the words as the threat they were likely meant to be.

The day had started with Jamie thinking his life was taking a turn.

His life had taken a turn that was for sure.

But if Don's behavior and words mixed with the dread boiling in Jamie's gut were any indication, then that turn had definitely not been for the better.

Not at all.

Kirk sat in the recliner in his dark living room.

He hadn't heard from Jamie since the night before when the kid said they were heading to dinner. Kirk had texted him a couple times. Okay, he'd texted him *several* times, but Jamie hadn't answered.

He's grown.

He can take care of himself.

He doesn't need me stepping in as the hero all the time.

In fact, it's one of the things he hates the most.

Let him be.

Would he be freaking out if Jamie lived with a loving family and hadn't answered his texts?

That question didn't matter because Jamie *wasn't* living with a loving family. He was living with Don fucking Carter who Kirk believed with every bone in his body was a pedophile, if not a rapist and murderer.

"Fuck!" Kirk slammed the recliner leg rest down and planted his feet on the floor before resting his head in both hands. He'd never felt so damn helpless in his life.

Kirk scrolled through the contacts on his phone. Could call Elliot. His partner was a good guy, knew Kirk was gay, and would probably have some advice. But Kirk had spent the better part of five whole days with Elliot and really didn't feel like dragging the new guy into his mess. Plus, Elliot didn't exactly know Kirk had been seeing Jamie. Trying to explain how Kirk and Jamie had gone from cop and victim to something more when Kirk wasn't even sure of how it happened wasn't where he wanted to put his energy at the moment.

Sam. Better to reach out to Sam. He knew Jamie, knew Kirk, and more importantly, Sam knew Don Carter.

Kirk thumbed his phone screen and waited for Sam to answer.

"Fuck, Kirkland, it's four thirty in the morning. What's wrong?" Sam growled through the phone.

Kirk pulled the phone from his ear to check the time. He hadn't realized it was so damn early. Or late in Kirk's case, since he hadn't been to bed.

"Sorry, man." Kirk hesitated slightly before continuing. "I'll owe you one. But it's Jamie."

Kirk heard shuffling on the other end of the phone line and

what sounded like Sam moving around. "Sorry, had to move rooms so I didn't wake Zach. What's going on?"

Kirk sighed. "Jamie decided to take kind-hearted Don Carter up on an offer to live with him. Go to dinner and basketball games, help around the house, be sort of a live-in companion of sorts in exchange for the older man's help paying for college."

"Why the hell would Jamie do that? That sounds fishy and scammy and all sorts of bad."

"Don fed Jamie some story about a long-lost grandson and Jamie fell for it. He wants so badly to prove he can survive without his parents that he would believe anything Don told him." Kirk pinched the bridge of his nose as he spoke.

"Plus, Don isn't someone he's interested in romantically. Don isn't someone who has seen Jamie at his worst. So staying with Don and letting *him* help was much more desirable in Jamie's eyes than staying with you." Sam sighed. "So, aside from a really stupid decision on Jamie's part, what else has you so worried?"

"He texted last night before they headed to dinner. Said he'd text again once they were home. But he never did. And he's not answered the texts I've sent him since." Kirk stood and began to pace.

"Have you been waiting up all damn night for the kid to text you?" Sam chuckled.

"Yeah, I have. I know it sounds crazy, Stein, but my gut has been churning over Carter long before Jamie ever got involved. And now it's about to boil over. Don is a bad guy with a lot of power. He's convinced we can't touch him, and he's determined to get whatever he wants, whenever he wants."

"And the fact that he can do all of this right under the law's nose is even more enticing to a guy like Carter." Sam cursed. "Okay, I see your point. Jamie could be in real danger. But we have no reason to go busting into Carter's house. He doesn't have a place of employment, so the best we can do is keep watch for the slightest mess up and bring him in. But honestly, that attorney of his is a damn shark, and she will eat us alive if we do anything outside of protocol or off the books."

Kirk paused in his pacing. Eyes closed and face lifted to the ceiling, he took a deep breath. "Can we trace Jamie's phone? See where it is?" Kirk knew the answer before Sam even spoke.

"I mean, if you had a tracking app or something on the phone, sure. Outside of that, we'd have to get the department involved. And we have no hard and fast evidence that warrants tracking the kid's phone." Sam paused. "Plus, if something comes from this situation as far as a court case, we can't use anything as evidence if we don't have a warrant."

"Damn it," Kirk huffed and gritted his teeth. "So what the hell do I do?"

"Catch up with Jamie at work or the center. Keep an eye on Don. I'll make sure the guys know to watch for Jamie and Don and anything weird if they see them in the restaurant. But aside from that, there's not a ton you can do."

"I can't just sit around and wonder what's going on while Jamie may be hurt or in danger." Kirk struggled to control his anger.

"Unless you want to lose your job and find yourself on the other end of Carter's power, I think that's all you *can* do, man. It sucks, but it's reality." Sam sighed. "I gotta go back to bed. I'm supposed to be at work in about three hours."

Kirk closed his eyes and blew out a long breath. "Yeah, man, I get it. Sorry again for waking you."

"No worries." Sam lowered his voice as he moved back through the house. "Listen, I'm not saying you don't have reason to worry. I'm just not sure what options you have at this point."

"I know you're right." Kirk flopped down onto the couch and curled up where Jamie had been cozied up not so long ago. "You only put words to what I already knew. Thanks, man."

"Keep in touch, yeah?"

"Will do," Kirk agreed and thumbed the phone screen to end

the call. Pulling the blanket from the back of the couch, the one Jamie had insisted he didn't need the first night Kirk had brought him to the house to do laundry, Kirk held the soft material close to his chest and breathed in deeply. "Damn it, Jamie, what's going on? I want to think you're just busy and getting settled in. But everything about Don Carter makes my head scream that's not the case. Can you just let me know you're okay?" Kirk whispered his plea into the darkness and clutched his phone tightly in his grip as if he could will Jamie to contact him.

J amie's eyes popped open, and he stared at the ceiling for several moments, trying to get his bearings. He was warm and comfortable, so he'd likely found a place to crash, but for the life of him he couldn't remember who had taken him in.

His mind cycled through the day and night before, but he remembered very little of either. Suddenly, his brain stuttered to a stop, and he sat up with the blankets clutched to his chest. Barely breathing and his heart pounding, Jamie wildly took in the room.

His room.

In Don Carter's house.

Bits and pieces came to his mind. Don had offered Jamie a place to stay and help paying for college. The scenario had seemed perfect, but Jamie's gut rolled and told him something was definitely wrong.

Physically and situationally.

Vaulting from bed, Jamie barely made it to the wastebasket in time before losing the contents of his stomach. Upon finishing,

Jamie made his way back to bed on wobbly legs with a pounding head.

What the hell had happened?

Something had gone wrong.

Why couldn't he remember?

Jamie searched for his phone. On the bedside table. Under the blankets. On the floor. Beneath the bed. In the pockets of his jeans and coat.

Where the hell had he left his phone?

He fell back onto the bed and pulled up the covers to ward off the shivering.

What was wrong with him?

A knock sounded on his door.

While Jamie contemplated not answering, he shrunk deeper into the covers when the door clicked open and Don's head appeared. "Good morning, my sleepy boy."

Jamie's stomach threatened a revolt again.

Don.

Something about Don was wrong.

"I'm sick. Why do I feel so sick?"

"Seems my boy can't handle wine very well." Don smiled as he entered the room and placed a tray on Jamie's bedside table. "I'm not surprised that you have a terrible hangover this morning."

"No, I've had hangovers. This is different. Like, my brain is all foggy. I barely remember anything." Jamie grabbed the bottle of water from the tray and chugged it.

"You moved in here yesterday. We went to dinner. You got highly inebriated on very fine wine. I brought you home. And here we are." Don shrugged as he poured steaming hot water over a tea bag in a mug. "It's up to you, but do you think you can handle work today?"

Jamie processed the question. He felt like shit. The thought of working a whole shift made his body tremble. "I don't think work is going to happen today. I hate to call off, but I don't think I could stay upright."

Don smiled and nodded. "Good boy. I agree. A day home to relax is probably best." Don sat on the edge of the bed, and Jamie inched closer to the headboard. "Honestly, I don't think you really *need* that job any longer. You've got me to take care of you now. I don't need my boy in a food service job. There's plenty of service you can offer here." Don winked.

Jamie fought the urge to gag. The ominous feelings he'd had about Don the evening before were back and multiplying tenfold. The car ride to the restaurant played through his head.

Don's story about Alec.

The truth about Don not having a grandson.

Don making him leave his phone.

Trying to keep his voice from shaking, Jamie swallowed hard. "Oh, hey, I can't find my phone. I need to charge it."

"Don't worry about it." Don chucked him on the shoulder. "I'll get you a newer one. A better one."

Jamie masked his unease with a nervous chuckle. "Sounds good, but all my contacts and information are on that phone. Sort of need it."

"Nonsense. No one in your past is that important. Think of what your family did to you. You admitted you were sort of a loner and didn't really have a lot of friends at the teen center or the restaurant. This is your chance to make a new start, a fresh beginning." Don laid a hand on Jamie's knee. "As soon as you're feeling better, we'll get the best phone available. Nothing is too good for my boy."

Jamie's nostrils flared in anger and fear. "Sounds good." He nodded. "But I don't think quitting my job is the best idea. I mean, you helping with school is great, but I'll still need money, and I won't be living here forever. I need to stay employed for future job opportunities."

Don's face flushed, and he raised a brow. "My dear boy, why

would you not stay here forever? My home is yours now. And I can buy or provide absolutely everything you need. You don't seem to understand what an amazing gift I can give you."

"And what's in it for you?" Jamie's words shot from his mouth before he could remind himself it was likely best to keep Don calm.

Don smiled.

A smile that sent shivers down Jamie's spine and convinced him he was in a very bad situation.

"You, my dear boy. *You* are what's in it for me."

"You just like paying for college and keeping a young guy in your guestroom?" Jamie squinted his eyes as he studied Don.

"For now, yes." Don reached a hand toward Jamie's face as if to cup his cheek, but Jamie jerked away. "Until you recognize the true nature of what we could share, I'll be happy to just help you succeed and keep you happy."

"What if I never recognize it? Never want to share that with you?" Jamie's mind spun in erratic circles. How had Don gone from the sweet, flirty, harmless older man who visited him at the restaurant to a psycho who wanted to lock Jamie in his house and make him...well, Don hadn't actually spelled out what he wanted to make Jamie do, but Jamie had a pretty good idea it was something he had no interest in doing.

"My dear boy, you will. You will. Don't worry." Don grabbed Jamie's hand and squeezed. "I can be *very* persuasive."

Was this what had happened with Alec? Did Don keep Alec the way he intended to keep Jamie?

Fuck.

Jamie needed to call Kirk.

Kirk.

Jamie's fuzzy mind brought Kirk's warnings to the forefront. But he'd been a punk ass kid refusing to listen to reason or advice. Hell bent on proving Kirk wrong, and proving he could take care of himself, had created a shit storm mess of epic proportions.

How the hell would he contact Kirk?

How would he get away from Don?

Offering Don his best fake-it-til-you-make-it smile, Jamie reached for the tea. Sipping the strong liquid helped to calm his stomach.

He needed time to think.

To plan.

"Could you call work for me? Let them know I'm not feeling well." Jamie batted his lashes and tried to look as innocent as possible. He'd keep Don calm and happy; make the guy think he'd accepted the situation. Keep up the charade and buy time to devise a plan.

"Of course, my boy." Don patted Jamie's hand. "I'll call them. Why don't you finish your tea and toast, take a warm shower, and then rest some more?"

"That sounds great." Jamie reached for the toast. "Will you be around today?"

"I'm always around, Jamie. I'll always be here. Don't ever doubt that." Don stood from the edge of the bed and frowned. "I left Alec alone too much. I won't do that to you."

"Great," Jamie muttered through a small smile. "It will be nice to not be alone."

"I know, my boy. I know." Don nodded and left the room.

FORTY-EIGHT HOURS LATER, A GROGGY JAMIE REALIZED DON MUST have put something in his drinks or on his food. Jamie had never felt so disoriented in all his life. No hangover had ever been so bad or lasted so long.

Between bouts of drug-induced lethargy and confusion, Jamie found time to think over his situation.

Don informed Jamie that he didn't have to work for the next several days and could make the decision about going back to work when he was feeling better. While that gave Jamie time to think about how to escape, he also knew it took away his chance to see other people and let them know he was in trouble. Which, of course, was exactly what Don wanted.

Jamie asked a couple more times about his phone, but Don got angrier with each request, so Jamie dropped it.

"I'll get you the best phone money can buy when I feel like you're ready to accept and appreciate this for what it is. A new start and a fresh beginning." Don had leaned down to kiss his head, and Jamie had swallowed the urge to vomit.

Jamie's gut told him he didn't have much time before Don lost patience and started expecting more. He feared being put in compromising situations while drugged. He trembled thinking of poor Alec, a boy he didn't even know. Had Alec been drugged? Mentally, physically, and emotionally abused? Raped? Jamie's head and heart warned that it wouldn't be long before he was in the same situation.

To hell with that.

Maybe Don was getting sloppy?

Maybe Don thought Jamie was more like Alec?

But no way in hell would he let Don keep him as a prisoner and sex slave. Not going to happen. Jamie felt for Alec. Had the boy had taken his own life, after being locked in Don's house and forced to do who knows what?

I need to find my phone.

Jamie knew finding his phone was the key to reaching Kirk.

But how?

Where?

Maybe if I can't find my phone, I can contact the police department? Or call someone at the restaurant? Call 911?

Jamie's gaze strayed to the phone. Had the phone been accessible the whole time? Why had Jamie not thought to use it? He reached a shaky hand toward the receiver and held the phone to his ear.

Nothing.

Dead.

Window?

Jamie glanced toward the windows of his room.

Bars?

Don had fucking bars on the windows?

Jamie closed his eyes against the onslaught of terror filling his mind.

Plan. *Make a damn plan.*

First, don't eat or drink anything that wasn't sealed or made by him.

Second, check the other phones in the house.

Third, were bars on every single window?

Fourth, find times when Don wasn't watching every single move and look for his phone.

Five, call Kirk.

Kirk.

Jamie had been so against Kirk being his savior, but now Kirk was the only thing Jamie could put his faith in.

No, put faith in yourself, as well.

Damn straight.

Jamie was wrong, and he may need Kirk more than he wanted to admit.

But he would not lay around and let Don fucking Carter drug him and rape him. He would *not* be his boy or his slave. He would save himself and make sure Don couldn't do this shit to any other person.

10

"God damn it," Kirk growled and held his head in both hands.

"Whoa, settle there, partner." Elliot glanced toward Kirk and frowned. "What's up?"

Kirk stared at Elliot for a moment. "You know that kid we took from the domestic dispute a while back?"

Elliot seemed to scan his brain for a moment before nodding. "Yeah, his father was beating the shit out of him?"

"Yeah, that's the one. His name is Jamie. We've sort of been seeing each other." Kirk glared at Elliot waiting for his surprise or disgust.

Elliot just shrugged. "Okay?"

"Well, he moved in with a guy, and I've not heard from him since." Kirk pinched the bridge of his nose.

"So, he broke up with you?" Elliot winced. "Sorry, man."

"No," Kirk huffed. "I mean, I don't think so. The guy he moved in with is a former suspect in a missing person case. I don't trust him. At all. But Jamie was so sure the offer would turn his life around."

"And you've not heard from him since he moved in with the guy? Not a single word?" Elliot raised a brow.

"Got one text saying he was at the house and would text after they went to dinner. Then nothing since." Kirk shoved a hand through his hair.

"And who were you just calling?"

"Called his phone, went straight to voicemail. Called his work, he's been off for days. They say he's been calling in sick." Kirk closed his eyes. "He's not been seen or heard from since the evening he moved in with Don Carter."

"Don Carter? I know that name. Why?" Elliot frowned.

"You weren't on the force yet, but I'm sure you heard about the case. Department investigating too many suspects, and Carter's attorney got him off on reasonable doubt even though we all knew he had something to do with the kid's disappearance. Huge fuck up of a case."

"Yeah, I do remember that." Elliot nodded. "Okay, so seems you have reason to be worried about the kid. Anywhere else he'd go?"

"I already checked the teen center. No one there has seen him."

"And you can't officially go to Carter's house without proof or evidence or a warrant...you could lose your job."

"At this point, I'm almost ready to say screw my job and go over there." Kirk gritted his teeth. "Something is wrong. I know it."

"You losing your job or being caught up in a legal battle won't help Jamie." Elliot paused. "What if we watched Carter's house for a while? I mean, if we've got downtime on a shift we could park nearby and watch for anything suspicious and nail his ass."

"You'd be willing to do that?" Kirk studied his partner.

"We park different places and watch people all the time. We'll take our lunch and any dead time on shift we'll settle near the Carter residence."

"Yeah, that's good. Nothing we haven't done before, just a different location."

Not the best plan, but at least it was something.

Too bad the next four days were littered with massive amounts of calls and Kirk never once had a moment to check out Carter's house.

By the time Kirk came off another five-day stint, he was positive he was going insane. He told himself he'd sleep and then stake out Carter's house himself.

I won't leave until I see Jamie and know he's safe. My job, my reputation, my future be damned. I can't sit by and watch Carter destroy another life. Especially not Jamie's.

JAMIE SET HIS PLAN INTO MOTION.

Jamie befriended the housekeeper and helped her around the kitchen. She spoke zero English and seemed scared to death of Carter, but she let Jamie sneaks bites of food here and there. He only ate food he'd seen prepared. Bottled water was his best friend. And tea or coffee only if he made it himself.

"Have some wine with me," Don had murmured at Jamie's ear one evening while Jamie washed his hands at the kitchen sink.

Jamie's disgust covered both his feelings toward drinking wine with Don *and* his feelings about the older man making such an intimately overt gesture. "Nah, no more wine for me. I still don't feel that great. I'm going to stick with water."

A disgruntled Don huffed away.

The next day, Jamie roamed the residence looking for house phones. He only found one other than the one in his bedroom. The phone in the living room was also dead.

His search for phones allowed him to also check the windows. No bars on the windows in the dining room, but he'd need a very tall ladder to even hope to reach those. Several other windows were without bars, but even if Jamie were to lift one and crawl out, they were blocked by a cage type apparatus. To the commoner, the cage looked intended to keep burglars out, but Jamie had a bad feeling they were meant to keep a person inside.

Trapped.

"What's with the bars on all the windows? And the cages? Aren't those like some sort of fire hazard? How are occupants getting out if there's a fire?" Jamie feigned interest one evening while pretending to enjoy dinner with Don.

"Ah, just a precaution in order to protect my belongings. In case of a fire, the security system would disengage the bars and cages." Don stared at Jamie for several moments. "But no worries, my boy. This house is specially equipped to be fireproof in all situations. Even a fire in the walls or another room would be snuffed out before anyone would even notice it. State of the art and only the best for my home and my belongings."

Jamie swallowed the feeling of dread and forced himself to finish his meal. He knew he would need his strength in the days to come if he wanted to best Don and save himself.

After several days of baby-stepping his plan, Jamie realized he would have to act fast. Don had announced from Jamie's bedroom door. "We're going on a trip, my dear boy. Pack your bags."

"What? Why? Where are we going?" Jamie had worked hard to fight the panic clawing up his throat.

"I'm tired of the poking, prodding, and intruding around here. You and I need a break. A place to ourselves to get to know each other better." Don stalked toward the bed like a tiger stalking his prey. "I'm a very patient man, but even *I* have my limits."

Jamie's fear went into overdrive. "Where are we going? When are we leaving? What about school? Classes start soon." He scooted as far away from Don as possible. "Who is intruding? No one ever comes here, and we barely ever go out."

"That's just it, my boy. I want to take you out, show you off, and spoil you. But here, too many eyes are watching." Don reached for Jamie's bent knee and licked his lips. "We'll go somewhere tropical. Our own private beach, clothing optional, and get that beautiful body of yours warmed pink from the sun. No one will know where we are."

"C-classes. Classes s-start soon." Jamie's words trembled.

"You can push classes back a semester and double up this summer." Don squeezed his knee. "You don't need a college education now that you're with me. I can provide you with anything and everything your heart desires."

My heart desires a college education. And to get away from you. To survive whatever psycho hell is going on here. To find Kirk and never let him go.

Jamie forced a smile and swallowed thickly. "Sounds good. Nice warm beach, yeah." Jamie nodded. "When will we leave?"

"I have appointments with my attorney and my physician tomorrow."

"So you'll be going out?" Jamie knew his words sounded too excited. "Want me to go with you?"

"Don't be silly. My people come to me. As long as both appointments go well, we can leave as early as tomorrow night. Maybe early the next morning." Don hefted himself from the mattress and cupped Jamie's cheek. "My dear sweet boy. I'll give you the moon and stars. You have no idea how good you have it and how good we'll be when you finally let me in."

Jamie's entire body clenched to avoid trembling at Don's words. "Just give me some time."

"I've waited long enough. It's time you return some of my hospitality." Don gripped Jamie's chin. "Pack your bags. I'll come for you tomorrow when it's time to leave."

Don left the bedroom, and Jamie sagged against his pillows for a split second before his brain was screaming, "No time to waste!" He needed to find his phone and find it now.

Jamie feigned sleep when Don popped into his bedroom the next morning.

"Good morning, sleepy boy." Don sat on the edge of Jamie's bed and traced his finger along the young man's cheek.

Jamie fluttered his lashes and pretended to wake. "Huh? What time is it?"

"I'm heading out, but I'll be back soon. Get up and get packed."

Jamie moaned. "I don't really feel all that great."

"Even more reason to get a move on and get us to a tropical location so you can rest, relax, and soak up some sun." Don's hand traveled from Jamie's shoulder down to cup his ass.

"Gonna sleep a little longer," Jamie mumbled and rolled over in hopes of protecting himself from Don's roaming hands.

"I expect you packed by the time I get home. Don't let me down."

Don's warning hung in the air long after the man had left the room. Jamie waited a full thirty minutes after hearing Cliff pull the car from the garage before he rolled from under the covers. He was fully dressed and had been awake for several hours before Don came for his morning visit. He had very little time to search the house for his phone before the housekeeper arrived. Jamie also knew he had to make his roaming and searching look as innocent as possible because, although he hadn't *seen* the cameras, he knew without a doubt that Don had cameras monitoring the house.

Jamie strolled through the house, singing and dancing and pretending to look at a magazine and tossed his backpack on the dining room table in hopes that it would look like he was packed and just killing time. Pleading with the universe that he was hidden in shadows enough not to be seen, he quickly slipped into Don's office. If Jamie wasn't successful in the office, his next stop was the basement. Both places Don had warned him to stay away from.

Don's office was clearly the center of the house's operations. At least fifteen video monitors sat in row upon row watching every move made in the house. Jamie shook off anger and disgust when he recognized the view of his bed and his shower.

"This ends today you fuckin' creep," Jamie whispered and began to search desk drawers for his phone. The bottom drawer of the rich mahogany desk looked to be the largest but was surprisingly shallow and strangely empty, but had a velvet bottom unlike the other drawers Jamie had searched. He pushed on the floor of the drawer and jerked his hand back when the flat surface shifted.

"What the hell?" Jamie tipped the velvet-covered material to the side and found a hidden compartment. "Bingo. Tell me this is my jackpot." Jamie rifled through the contents in the bottom of the drawer. By the time he'd pulled out all the items and placed them carefully on Don's desktop, he had quite the collection.

Three plastic baggies with what appeared to be locks of hair. Two wallets. Multiple identification cards and passports. A loaded handgun along with enough loose bullets to reload at least once. And several phones.

Jamie's body teemed with panic and fear, but his mind remained calm. Having many phones to choose from upped his chances of being able to call for help even if one of the devices wasn't his. But with all that had gone wrong lately, luck was on Jamie's side when he sifted through the phones and found his own. It was turned off. Jamie held his breath as he powered it on.

Would there be enough battery?

The phone screen came to life and Jamie nearly wept with relief.

He found his recent calls and quickly thumbed Kirk's number.

Jamie held the phone to his ear and prayed Kirk would pick up.

His plan wasn't fail proof and depended on Kirk answering.

What if Kirk had given up on him?

Don't be stupid. If he doesn't answer you can call 911. Kirk isn't the only one who can save you. Save yourself, dumbass.

Jamie chuckled at the absurdity of his thoughts during a psycho-crazy situation that seemed better for the plot of a movie than real life.

The phone rang a third time.

If it went to voicemail, Jamie would have no choice but to call 911. His heart hurt to think Kirk wasn't worried about him. They hadn't had much time to work on whatever it was they had developing, but Jamie believed they had something.

By the fourth ring, Jamie's heart gave up hope.

11

——————

Kirk's phone rang as he headed toward Don Carter's block. He'd been parking his car in different spots around the vicinity to watch Carter's house, but the day before he was pretty sure Don had spotted him. Today Kirk drove a buddy's car and planned to park in a completely different location.

"Kirkland," he barked into the phone.

"It's Stein."

"Go ahead." Kirk's fist gripped the phone.

"You know the other day when you said Don fed Jamie some story about a long lost grandson?"

"Yeah." Kirk waited for Sam to get to the point.

"Well, it's been bouncing in my head and I finally figured it out. Carter was an only child, never married, parents deceased. He has no family, definitely no long lost grandson."

Kirk's gut clenched. "I knew the grandson story was a bunch of bullshit." Kirk pulled the phone away from his ear when he heard another call coming in. "Jamie," he breathed in a relieved and fearful whisper. "Shit, Sam, I gotta go. Jamie is calling." Kirk thumbed the screen to end one call and answer the other, hoping he was getting to Jamie's call in time.

"Jamie?" Kirk's words were loud and filled with emotion.

"Kirk, I'm in trouble." Jamie's words were rushed. "What was the name of the kid who disappeared? The one you thought Don was involved with?"

Kirk scanned his mind for several seconds and his brain fought with answering the question and finding out where Jamie was and if he was okay. "Um, Alec. Alec Swanson." Kirk pressed the accelerator and sped toward Carter's. "Jamie, where are you? Are you okay?"

"I'm at Carter's. Things are really fucked up. Can you come get me?" Jamie's words caught on a sob.

"I'm on my way now. Just sit tight." Kirk gunned the car even faster. "Are you hurt?"

"I'm not hurt. Just hurry," Jamie whispered. "Kirk, be careful. He's a fucking psycho."

"I'm almost there," Kirk promised. "Stay on the line with me, okay?"

There was a scuffle and different voice in the background of the call. "Jamie?"

"Shit, Kirk, he's here. He's back early. I gotta go. Please hurry."

The line went dead.

Kirk had never understood what it meant when someone would say their heart was outside of their body. But he got it. He totally got it now. Knowing Jamie was in trouble, knowing Don was there, knowing Jamie had reached out, and he may not make it to help in time was the worst form of torture.

Kirk glanced up to see red lights in his rearview. He'd never been so glad to be pulled over for speeding. Kirk put an arm out the window motioning them to follow him. Then he called Sam.

"Sam, call the department. I'm on my way to Carter's. Jamie called and said he's in trouble. Don walked in on the call, and

Jamie hung up. I'll need backup." Kirk shouted his words into the phone and hung up before Sam could even respond.

Skidding to a stop in front of Don Carter's residence, Kirk jumped from the car and flashed his badge at the officers who were tailing him.

"Young kid, age nineteen, is inside. Called and said he's in trouble. The homeowner is dangerous and very likely highly armed." Kirk pulled his gun from its holster.

The officers exchanged looks of disbelief.

"Look, you remember the court case that went to shit when the kid disappeared, and Don Carter was let go on reasonable doubt?" Kirk headed toward the house, giving the officers no choice but to follow.

They drew their own weapons and nodded.

"Well, this is Carter's house, and he's got another kid in there. If we're not careful and quick then this kid may end up missing or dead the same as Alec Swanson." Kirk studied the perimeter of the house and wished like hell he knew where Jamie was located. A storm cellar door caught Kirk's eye and he headed toward it. "Look, I've got backup coming, but I'd appreciate if you'd call this one in and cover me."

"We should wait for backup," the younger officer stammered.

"You *are* my backup for now. I'm not waiting when a kid's life is in danger." Kirk fired at the lock and quickly opened the door. He and the two officers climbed down the dark and damp stairs only to find another door.

Clearly the storm cellar entrance was no longer used for safety from storms.

Kirk shot the second door lock and gestured for silence when he pulled the door open, revealing a narrow dirt floor hallway.

"Here, take the radio. We'll go this way, and you go that way. Radio if you find anything." The older officer handed the walkie to Kirk. "Dispatch says backup is only two minutes away."

Kirk went into complete and total cop mode. His brain and

body did at least. His heart, on the other hand, was clenched in fear and needed to see Jamie whole and unharmed.

A crash sounded above and to the left. Kirk jogged from the dirt lined hallway, through a door, and up a set of stairs that brought him out into a utility room of sorts. Having no clue of the house's layout or where Jamie was located meant Kirk was basically blind. He kept his gun drawn, his eyes on constant look out, and his ears listening for any sound that could offer a clue.

Something fell over or was knocked over somewhere ahead of him. Finding the kitchen clear, Kirk kept to the perimeter, hugging the walls, as he slowly inched forward.

A gunshot rang out, and Kirk's heart clawed its way to his throat.

Someone screamed and three more shots rang out.

Then all was silent.

Kirk crept forward, gun still drawn, heart barely beating, his chest tight with the breath he was holding. Down a long hallway, Kirk saw a solitary door open and smelled the scent of gunpowder. Wanting nothing more than to rush down the hallway and into the room, Kirk forced himself to stay on guard and inch toward where he thought Jamie and Carter might be.

But who would he find with the gun?

Who had screamed?

"You fucking sick son of a bitch." Jamie's words rang out clear and loud from beyond the door.

Kirk's knees nearly gave way, and he fought away the tears that stung at his eyes.

"Jamie?" Kirk called out.

"Kirk, I'm in here."

Kirk walked through the door and found Jamie standing with a gun pointed at Carter.

Carter moaned and writhed on the office floor, clutching his bloody knee.

The two officers rushed into the room, followed by the backup.

Kirk sighed in relief and holstered his gun. Walking to Jamie, Kirk took the pistol from the kid's shaky grip and laid it on the desk. Then he wrapped Jamie in his arms and held him tight.

Jamie collapsed and cried against his shoulder. "I'm so sorry."

Kirk pulled back from Jamie enough to lift his chin and meet his gaze. "You have absolutely *nothing* to be sorry about."

"Officer Kirkland, we need to secure the area and transport Mr. Carter," one of the backup officers spoke softly from beside Kirk and Jamie.

Never letting go of Jamie, Kirk fought the urge to kick Carter in the face as he led his fellow officers into the hallway.

Kirk kept his voice low. "Listen, that man was a previous suspect and is now a current suspect. Do *not* let him out of your sight. Do *not* mess up the crime scene."

"No worries, Kirk. I'll help keep an eye on things." Sam clapped Kirk on the shoulder.

Kirk gave Sam a questioning look and his former colleague shrugged. "Special privileges come with having friends in high places. I'm not *on* the case, but I'll be sure everything is by the book and followed to a T."

Kirk gave Sam a nod and relieved smile. "Good to hear." He turned to the other officers. "Jamie needs to give a statement. I want the paramedics to draw blood to test for foreign substances, as well."

Jamie's head shot up from resting on Kirk's arm. "I'm positive he was giving me something. I didn't start feeling better or knowing what was going on until I stopped eating or drinking anything that wasn't sealed."

Kirk winced and pulled Jamie's head back to rest on his shoulder. "Blood draw, Jamie needs checked out, he gives his statement, and then he's done for now. I'll bring him back to the station within the next couple days if more is needed."

Even with Kirk barking orders and demands it took well over three hours before Jamie was medically released and his lengthy statement was given. Kirk kept an eagle eye on Jamie as well as the authorities as they roped off the crime scene and began gathering evidence. Any other time, Kirk would have been pumped and salivating at the chance to work the scene that would bring about Carter's downfall, but all Kirk wanted to do was take Jamie home and make sure the kid was okay.

"You ready to go?" Kirk sat next to Jamie at the kitchen table as the paramedic finished paperwork at the counter.

"Never been so ready to go somewhere in my entire life." Jamie smiled and laid his head on Kirk's shoulder. "Do you think I'll ever get my phone back?"

"It may be part of evidence for a while. But we can get you set up with something in the meantime."

"Don wanted to get me a new phone and it creeped me out. You want to get me a new phone and it sounds like the best idea ever."

Kirk smiled and put an arm around Jamie. "Then a new phone it is." He kissed the young man's head. "Come on, let's go."

Kirk helped Jamie into the car and drove down the street. Within moments, Jamie's eyes were fluttering shut.

"I'm sorry I needed you to rescue me again."

"Don't give me that shit," Kirk growled. "You had Carter down for the count before I even walked into that office. You didn't *need* me to bring him down. I'm glad I could be there, but you handled that all on your own."

Jamie smiled as his eyes shut again. "Yeah, I guess you're right. I was pretty bad-ass."

Kirk chuckled and reached for Jamie's hand as they drove toward home.

"How 'bout you shower while I fix some food? I'll jump in the shower once I've got something started." Kirk's suggestion brought a smile and nod from Jamie.

"Food sounds great. I had to skip so much at Don's for fear he'd put something in it. I feel like I could eat a horse." Jamie stretched and took off his coat. "And a shower without being scared to death of some creeper watching or walking in on me sounds like just the medicine I need."

Kirk winced at Jamie's words and hesitated only a moment before voicing his concern. "Did Don hurt you?"

Jamie shook his head sadly. "No, but his demeanor changed the second I was in his house. Like, I was shocked at how quickly he changed his story and his attitude."

"Well, once he had you there, he probably thought he'd won and there wasn't anything you could do about it." Kirk stood beside Jamie at the sink.

"He took my phone that first night. Was very verbal about not wanting me in touch with you or anyone for that matter." Jamie shivered and leaned into Kirk's arm resting around his shoulders.

"I don't know how long Alec was with Don, but I can't imagine the nightmare it must have been. Don started cutting me off from the world within hours of being at his house. I know he was using chemical substances of some sort to keep me dazed and confused. He wasn't physically or verbally violent, yet his words and actions were scary and threatening all the same." Jamie burrowed against Kirk's chest. "I think he was very close to making the situation sexual. Told me he'd been as patient as he could be and that I needed to do my part."

Kirk moved Jamie so the young man was nestled between his legs, Jamie's back on Kirk's chest. "It killed me when I never heard back from you. I was going insane. I decided, fuck my job *and* my future, I was planning to bust him no matter what."

"What do you mean?"

"I'd started staking out his house waiting for him to make one wrong move."

"So, *that's* why he wanted to leave."

"He was leaving?"

"No, *we* were leaving. He was all agitated about poking, prodding, and intruding. That's why he wanted us to go to some tropical location, away from everyone else." Jamie was quiet for several moments. "If he'd gotten me out of the country...I'm not sure I would have known how to get away."

Kirk sighed and held him tighter. "He must have spotted me watching. Guess I wasn't as careful as I thought." He stood silently. "Don't spend time thinking of the what ifs. You were amazing. You didn't let Don get the best of you. He had no clue what he was getting himself into when he set his sights on you."

"I just can't stop thinking about what happened to Alec. And there had to be others. He had too many little trophies in that drawer." Jamie brought both hands up to cover his face. "He has to be put away so he can never do this to someone else."

"The department and prosecutors will do everything to make sure that happens this time." Kirk kissed the side of Jamie's neck.

"Have I told you how damn happy I am to have you here and safe in my arms?"

Jamie leaned into the kiss. "I'll listen to you tell me a million times."

"Go get a shower. I'll give you thirty minutes. Then you better be in my room ready to veg out and eat. We're doing nothing for the rest of the evening and maybe nothing for the next several days." Kirk walked Jamie toward the bathroom before returning to the kitchen.

"Hey, what's wrong?" Jamie entered Kirk's bedroom after his shower and found the other man leaning against the dresser, sobbing. He put his arms around Kirk's waist.

Kirk turned quickly and pulled Jamie into a full-body embrace. "Damn it, I'm sorry. I've been so fucking worried about you. Selfishly, I felt terrible, thinking you had decided you didn't want anything to do with me. Professionally, I knew something was wrong, and I was so scared you were going to be hurt."

Jamie's heart simultaneously broke and fluttered. "Shhh, it's okay, I'm okay."

"When I heard your voice on the phone, saying you needed help, I knew something was very wrong." Kirk continued to cry.

"Yeah, because you knew I was a punk ass kid who would never admit he needed someone unless it was life or death," Jamie tried to tease.

"When I heard those gun shots, I was so sure I was going to walk into that office and find you dead." Kirk shuddered and hugged Jamie even closer.

"Hey, I'm here. I'm fine." Jamie cupped Kirk's face in his palms. "It was scary as fuck, but I'm okay, *we're* okay."

"Do you still want there to be an us?"

Kirk's question struck at Jamie's heart.

Jamie kissed Kirk, sweeping his tongue along Kirk's lips. "Of course, I want there to be an us. What do you think kept me going and determined to get away from Don fucking Carter?"

Kirk laughed into the kiss. "How hungry are you?" He rocked his hips against Jamie's before clutching Jamie's ass and squeezing.

"I'm starving, but food can wait," Jamie breathed against Kirk's mouth.

"You sure?" Kirk continued to rock his hard length against Jamie's.

"More sure than I've ever been in my life."

"What do you want?" Kirk kissed along Jamie's jawline and nibbled at his ear.

"You. Any and every way I can get you." Jamie stepped back to strip his shirt over his head and shuck his pants and underwear. He paused and watched Kirk. "Um, were we not talking about the same thing? Get naked."

Kirk shook from his daze. "Sorry, you're just breathtaking. I was enjoying the show." Kirk stripped off his clothes and stood chest to chest with Jamie. Walking toward the bed, Kirk pushed Jamie backward until he fell upon the mattress. "Fucking hell, you are so damn gorgeous."

Kirk crawled on his knees until reaching Jamie's mouth, their rock-hard cocks rubbing together and taking his breath away. Kirk devoured Jamie's mouth, their tongues thrusting in the same rhythm as their hips.

Kirk trailed kisses down Jamie's throat, teased his tongue across pebbled nipples, placed tiny bites along Jamie's smooth abdomen, and breathed deeply when he reached Jamie's groin. Kirk buried his nose in Jamie's tight curls and cupped Jamie's balls in his hand. Tonguing the head of Jamie's cock, Kirk teased and lapped until Jamie was writhing in anticipation. Kirk opened wide and took Jamie's cock into his hot mouth.

"Fuuuuck," Jamie moaned and thrust his hips from the bed.

Kirk worked Jamie's cock over with his tongue and fist, but left him begging for more when he felt Jamie's balls draw up tight. "Not yet," Kirk growled. He moved his attention to Jamie's ass. Trailing his tongue from Jamie's balls to his hole, Kirk feasted upon his ass like a starving man at a buffet. Kirk thrust his tongue into Jamie's body several times.

Jamie jacked his cock.

Kirk reached up and batted his hand away. "You don't get to come yet."

Jamie moaned. "Then fuck me," he demanded.

Kirk licked a finger and probed at Jamie's hole gently. "Are you sure? Maybe we should take it slow this first time?"

Jamie spread his legs and opened himself completely to Kirk. "Fuck me, Kirk. I want your cock buried deep in my ass when I come."

Kirk reached for lube and a condom from the bedside drawer. "Look at you. Who knew you were such a hungry little bottom boy?"

Jamie rolled over and tackled Kirk onto his back. He reached for Kirk's throbbing dick and stroked it once, twice, before teasing Kirk's ass with a wet finger. "Don't ever doubt that I can and will top you better than you've ever dreamed," Jamie threatened.

Sounded more like a promise to Kirk's ears.

Kirk bucked and rolled Jamie to his back before attacking his mouth in the most intense, promising, hungry kiss he had ever experienced. "As fucking fabulous as that sounds, I'm perfectly fine with you being my greedy little bottom right now." Kirk grabbed the condom, made short work of the wrapper and rolled it down his pulsing dick before slathering himself with lube and smearing the liquid around and in Jamie's ass.

Kirk moved to the side of the bed so he could stand and pulled Jamie's ass to the edge of the mattress. "Don't touch yourself unless I tell you to."

"Bossy. I like it," Jamie teased only seconds before Kirk's cock nudged at Jamie's hole, making him gasp and moan. "Yes," Jamie hissed as Kirk pressed the blunt head of his dick against his tight center.

"Open for me, baby. Push against me and let me in." Kirk inched his way forward, closer and closer to burying himself balls deep in Jamie's sweet ass. "Fuck, you're so damn tight." Kirk continued to move bit by bit, holding his body tight, sweat forming on his brow when every instinct begged him to slam his cock deep.

Jamie pressed hard against the invasion of Kirk's thickness, gasped when Kirk's dick breached the final ring of resistance, and sank until his balls nestled against his ass.

Kirk took a moment to allow for adjustment and the catching of their breath.

"You okay?" Kirk ground out his words.

"I'd be a whole lot better if you'd fucking move," Jamie whined and rocked his ass.

Kirk pulled out slowly before thrusting in hard and deep. He leaned down and pulled Jamie into his arms while continuing to drive into Jamie's body over and over. "Fuck, never been this good. Gotta slow down, or it'll be over too fast."

"God damn, Kirk, I'm so close to coming. I'm not going to last very much longer." Jamie held tight to Kirk's shoulders and whimpered as Kirk filled his body.

"Touch yourself," Kirk growled and increased his rhythm.

Jamie reached for his cock, twisting and stroking until he exploded in long ropes of white between their bodies.

Kirk grasped Jamie's head and kissed him until his own orgasm ripped through him and he threw his head back with a roar. His cock pulsed deep one last time before he collapsed against Jamie's chest.

When both men had returned to earth, Kirk rolled from Jamie's body and disposed of the condom before grabbing a towel to wipe them both down. He climbed back into bed and cuddled beside Jamie.

"That was amazing. Thank you." Jamie whispered in Kirk's ear.

"Beyond amazing." Kirk rolled to face Jamie.

Jamie bit his lip and blushed. "I need to thank you for saving me. I didn't want to admit I needed saving and protecting back when you rescued me from my dad. And I didn't want to admit I'd screwed up with Don. But I see now that it's not all that bad to need a hero, and I'm happy you're mine." Jamie leaned in and kissed Kirk.

Kirk smiled into the kiss and let it deepen for several seconds before pulling back.

"I should thank you, as well." Kirk cupped Jamie's cheek in his hand.

"For what? I didn't do a damn thing." Jamie frowned.

"Shut up and let me thank you." Kirk pulled Jamie close for a kiss. "I didn't even realize I needed saving. I thought I was doing just fine on my own. I had a couple friends, my job, and a decent house. I was as happy as I figured I'd ever be. But then you came into my life and made it so much better than I ever dreamed."

Jamie's eyes welled with tears. "Maybe we should be saying a big thank you to the universe for saving us."

Kirk thumbed away Jamie's tear and pressed his forehead against Jamie's. "Here's to saving us."

EPILOGUE

"Hey, do you think we can meet up with the guys for brunch tomorrow?" Kirk called from the kitchen as Jamie worked on his homework Friday evening.

"Yeah, I can finish this assignment tonight. Brunch will be a nice little break before I start on the next one." Jamie mumbled back without tearing his eyes from his laptop.

Kirk smiled at Sam and handed him a beer. "Let's go out back. Don't want to disturb the student."

Sam and Kirk walked to the back of the house and sat on the steps. Jamie's winter session classes had ended a week ago, but the kid was neck deep in homework from spring session classes. The New York days were getting warmer and longer. Kirk's police work was the same as usual. Jamie had given up the job at the restaurant to focus completely on his studies although he made some money on the side creating apps with Zach and modeling here and there for Julian's clothing line.

"So, tell me about the case. Think it's going to hold up this time?" Sam took a long draw from the beer.

"From what I can tell, Jamie's statement and the fact that he pressed charges will help a lot. A lot of evidence was gathered from Don's place. The locks of hair, the phones, the wallets, the ID cards, the passports, all of those things are new evidence that can be used against him. He's got the same team of attorneys again, but a lot more is going against him this time around. Plus, there's no other suspect. Don is Numero Uno." Kirk swigged his beer. "Finding Alec, dead or alive, would be a big break in the case."

"Hate to think what that kid went through." Sam shook his head.

"If he's found dead then that's more evidence against Carter."

"Only if the body provides that evidence," Sam reminded.

"True." Kirk nodded. "But if Alec were found alive, would he be able to give enough information about his time with Carter to put Donny-boy away?" Kirk shrugged. "I want the kid alive, but I'd hate to think what he's been through."

"Yeah," Sam agreed. "So for now it's a wait and see with the Carter case?"

Kirk nodded.

"Do you think Jamie will have to testify?"

"Maybe, but I'm not sure." Kirk drank more of his beer and glanced over his shoulder at the house.

"He okay with doing it if it comes to that?" Sam raised his brows.

"Yeah, I think so. He wants Carter put away so he can't hurt anyone else."

"He still going to counseling?"

"Yeah, he goes and sometimes I go with him. It's good." Kirk lips settled into a soft, serene smile.

Jamie wandered to the back door. "You two want more beer?"

"Sure, thanks." Sam gestured with his bottle.

"Too bad. Until I can drink with the big boys, I'm not providing waiter service to you assholes." Jamie laughed and plopped his ass down next to Kirk. "But I'll give you my love for free."

"And I love your love," Kirk teased. "Just over a year, then you can have adult beverages." He bumped Jamie's shoulder.

"I can *have* adult beverages *now*." Jamie pursed his lips. "But living with an officer of the law means I have to toe the line."

"Or what?" Sam teased. "Does he get out the handcuffs and punish you like the bad little boy you really are?"

"Okay, that just sounds so wrong coming from you." Kirk laughed and nearly choked on his beer.

"Do you and Zach have some police and criminal fantasies you want to share?" Jamie batted his lashes at Sam.

Sam just laughed and finished his beer. "So, brunch tomorrow?"

Kirk and Jamie joined the laughter. "Yeah, we'll be there. Haven't seen all the guys in a while."

"Sounds good. See ya then." Sam descended the stairs and tossed his bottle in the recycle tub.

"You done with homework?" Kirk asked as he watched Sam walk to his car, which was parked on the street.

"For now, because my brain can't handle any more." Jamie leaned against Kirk.

"You know what I want? I want to take a bath and watch a movie cuddled on the couch with the man I love." Kirk tipped Jamie's chin and kissed him.

"That sounds divine. Lead the way." Jamie took Kirk's hand and let out a yelp when Kirk scooped him up in his arms. "Oh, my *hero*," Jamie teasingly crooned.

"Always," Kirk whispered in Jamie's ear before carrying him inside.

THE END

ALSO BY A.D. ELLIS

Ollie & Bash: On Cravenwood Block- a steamy, opposites-attract, roommates-to-lovers, boss/employee, age-gap M/M romance featuring a man not looking for love and a younger music director with no filter.

Holly Hills Christmas- Holly Hills Christmas is a steamy, feel-good, M/M age-gap holiday romance.

The Perfect Blend- A steamy, M/M age-gap, marriage of convenience, coffee shop romance

Perfect Timing is a steamy, M/M romance with an introverted, demisexual writer and a big, soft teddy bear of a nurse trying to navigate a love they've always dreamed of but most definitely weren't expecting.

Adore (Remington Place 1) is a steamy, age-gap, bi-awakening, dad's best friend M/M romance with a sassy smartass and a sexy silver fox. It's the first book in the Remington Place series and can be read as a stand-alone.

Crave (Remington Place 2) is a steamy, friends-to-lovers, fake relationship M/M romance with a virgin nursing student and a gruff, grumbly construction worker.

Desire (Remington Place 3) is a steamy, age-gap, hurt/comfort M/M romance featuring a heart-of-gold mechanic and a twink who's a lot stronger than he realizes. *Please note: This story has mention of sex trafficking and sexual abuse.*

Yearn (Remington Place 4)- a steamy, enemies-to-lovers, forced proximity M/M romance between two EMS workers who have hated each other for a decade.

Power Struggle is a steamy M/M, age-gap, forced proximity romance set in a small town. A twenty-year history, rival schools and jobs, and a hotel with only one bed make for a hot and heavy, sweet and sexy, HEA-guaranteed love story.

Take Me Home M/M age-gap, opposites-attract romance with plenty of steam and a scene that will make you appreciate camouflage and work boots

Let Love In M/M age-gap, forced proximity, dad's best friend, bisexual-awakening romance. Available on AUDIO!

Let Love Win M/M brother's best friend romance. Available on AUDIO!

Buried Secrets Romantic suspense stand-alone title. Available on AUDIO!

Silver in the City (3 books- meet the Silver crew you read about in Forged in the City) Available on AUDIO!

Forged in the City (3 books- a spin-off series from Silver in the City) Available on AUDIO

The BJ Boys Series (3 books, small town, big love) Available on AUDIO

Forever Better Together (friends to lovers) Available on AUDIO!

His Reluctant Cowboy (age gap, opposites attract, cowboy romance) Available on AUDIO!

What Blooms Beneath (LGBT Fantasy romance) Available on AUDIO!

Sawyer

(this was the first M/M I wrote and you may remember Sawyer and Luke being mentioned in Barrett & Ivan as well as in Ryker & Gavin)

The Something About Him series has been revamped with revised stories, updated blurbs, and spiffy new covers.

The series is available on ALL of your favorite book platforms!

Bryan & Jase

Brody & Nick

Barrett & Ivan

Braeton & Drew

Ryker & Gavin

Kade & Cameron

A.D.'s first stories (all male/female except <u>Sawyer</u> which is male/male) are in the Torey Hope and Torey Hope: The Later Years series. Find the 8 book box set HERE or you can find each individual title on Amazon.

For Nicky

Because of Beckett

Christmas in Torey Hope

Loving Josie

Decker

Sawyer

Zach

Kendrick

ABOUT THE AUTHOR

A.D. Ellis is an Indiana girl, born and raised. She spends much of her time in central Indiana teaching alternative education in the inner city of Indianapolis, being a mom to two amazing school-aged children, and wondering how she and her husband of almost two decades have managed to not drive each other insane. A lot of her time is also devoted to phone call avoidance and her hatred of cooking.

She loves chocolate, wine, pizza, and naps along with reading and writing romance. These loves don't leave much time for housework, much to the chagrin of her husband. Who would pick cleaning the house over a nap or a good book? She uses any extra time to increase her fluency in sarcasm.

ACKNOWLEDGMENTS

The biggest thank you has to go to Felice Stevens for inviting me to write in her world. Felice is a fabulous writer and to tell a story in her world is a true honor. Even though the world program was removed, I loved taking part in it and I really enjoyed writing Jamie and Kirk's story.

Thank you to the other talented authors writing in the world. Having my book and my name listed among such great writers is truly a privilege.

Thank you, Becky, for helping me get the New York information right! I'm glad you live in Indiana now, but I greatly appreciate your East Coast experience and background.

Thank you, JJ, for catching my errors and being a second set of eyes for me. I'm thinking you should hang that editor shingle soon. You'd have my vote.

To my dear beta readers. Your input, feedback, and encouragement has proven invaluable to me! I truly trust you all and value your opinions more than you'll probably ever understand. Thank you to my newest betas as well. When I needed fresh new eyes who had never read any of these characters you were there for me and helped me so much!

To my READERS!! You are what keeps me going. You are the reason I write some days. When I don't feel like I have it in me, I'll get a message or comment from a reader about how a story of mine has touched them, and *that* will be the inspiration and motivation for me to write. As long as these stories are in my head, I'll keep sharing them with you.

To the BLOGGERS who read and review and share my books!! You are beyond a shadow of a doubt some of the most dedicated and selfless people I've ever known! Thank you so much for being such a support to those of us who have stories to tell. I love BLOGGERS!

To my Juice Box ladies! Thank you so much for welcoming me into your crew and sharing your knowledge, experience, advice, and fun with me! Having some real-life authors/friends I can collaborate with is a great feeling. Dance parties, lunches, movies, videos, wine, painting, pizza...the list goes on and on! Thank you for letting me be a Juice Boxer!

Cheryl Brooks, thank you for working your magic on my blurbs.

To my fellow authors. Those of you who read my work, share your work with me, cross-promote with me, and offer advice and support, THANK YOU! You make this a little easier and enjoyable.

CONNECT WITH A.D. ELLIS

Follow my website http://www.adellisauthor.com or find me on Facebook

http://www.facebook.com/adellisauthor

If you want to get updates about releases, interviews, sales, giveaways, and more please sign up for my newsletter bit.ly/ADEllisNews

You can also find me on Twitter http://www.twitter.com/ADEllisAuthor